BLISS

THE FRENCH LIST

Bliss

CLARA MAGNANI

TRANSLATED BY
TERESA LAVENDER FAGAN

LONDON NEW YORK CALCUTTA

**PAP
TAGORE**
www.bibliofrance.in

This work is published with the support of the
Publication Assistance Programmes of the Institut français

Seagull Books, 2021

First published in French as *Joie* by Clara Magnani
© Sabine Wespieser éditeur, Paris, 2017

First published in English by Seagull Books, 2021
English translation © Teresa Lavender Fagan, 2021

ISBN   978 0 8574 2 880 6

British Library Cataloguing-in-Publication Data
A catalogue record for this book is available from the British Library.

Typeset by Seagull Books, Calcutta, India
Printed and bound in the USA by Integrated Books International

Because what you want is this life, and that one,
and another—you want them all. And you are quite right.

Miguel de Unamuno

* * *

Elvira

2014. A sunny September morning. My father was reading when his heart stopped. Just like that, without warning. A heart attack. No pain. No chemo or paralysis. No need to beg a Swiss doctor for a euthanasia pill costing over ten thousand euros. That was exactly the way he wanted to go. He said: '*Un bel morir tutta la vita onora*'—'a beautiful death honours all of life.' I was happy for him.

It was the end of summer in Rome. He was wearing his favourite kimono. Plum-coloured, with three yellow flowers. He had collapsed while sitting on the terrace of his flat. There was a plate of apricots in front of him. Sweet. He had eaten only half of one of them. The cleaning lady called me, beside herself. I was the only person she knew in Rome. When I arrived, the record he had been listening to was still playing. Gould continued to play the *Goldberg Variations* as if nothing had happened. I put my hand on his face. He was smiling. His eyes were wide open. I closed them.

The police and the ambulance arrived shortly afterwards. The men shrugged. Nothing out of the ordinary. Nothing to clarify. Condolences. They said they were going to take away the body for post-mortem formalities. Looking around him, one of the men whistled softly: '*Non è male questo posto . . .* this place isn't bad.'

I asked the cleaning lady to come back the following week. Then I sat on my father's chair and cried. Bach, too, was sad. Why did he die now? His life wasn't easy at first. He even had mild contempt for those he felt had been kissed by fortune. He had me late in life. Finally a little girl, who could have been his granddaughter. But at seventy, he felt oddly closer to twenty-five-year-olds, people of my generation, than forty-somethings. They didn't interest him. 'Make money, as much as you can, as quickly as you can, on the backs of others—that's their MO,' he would say. 'You, the younger ones, you know that the system is rotten and you aren't fooled. That's already something.'

Giangiacomo—Gigi, as everyone called him, including my mother, Irma. I kept thinking about the expression on his face when I found him. Calm. So calm. His head lying on the table. He looked like he was resting. He had been rereading one of his favourite books, *Quer pasticciaccio brutto de via Merulana* by Carlo Emilio Gadda. The novel that he couldn't make into a film. 'The greatest books resist film,' he told me one day. I didn't agree. 'What about Visconti? *Il gattopardo*? And Faenza's *I Vicerè*?' He didn't answer. One day, however, one of his friends had the same debate with him. '*Il Gattopardo*?' I heard his response. He thought the film was a bit *dolce*.

Gadda was languishing on the ground, covered in ants. I shook it. Put it back on the table. Gigi had always encouraged us children to dive into the book. But he talked about it so much that I felt I already knew the story. That week, I read it. In one sitting. It was indeed *un capolavoro*. A masterpiece. Did I think that because Gigi wasn't there any more, and I missed him? Would I have been more critical while he was alive? Just for the pleasure of disagreeing? In any case, today, it didn't matter. If only he could have lived another ten years. And to think that the walking corpse who doubles as the president is still alive in the Quirinale. Not fair.

A week later, I went back to Gigi's place to tidy his office . . . There were papers everywhere. He who hated paperwork . . . Suddenly, I came upon a manuscript. Printed text, carefully hidden under piles of bank statements, in the bottom drawer of his desk. It had been edited in red ink. Notations in the margin. Illegible notes. Was it a new filmscript? I read it over and over in search of clues. It was about someone named Clara. A Clara who dominated the text . . .

Clara?

I kept reading. Something told me that this woman must have existed. That she still existed, perhaps. How much had he altered her so she wouldn't be recognized? Was she really Belgian, as the text suggested? Strange. An Italian in love with a Belgian? The story began to draw me in. It wasn't a great work of literature, but it was the story of his life. Who knows? Maybe *the* great story of his life.

Gigi. What I loved about him was that he refused to behave like other parents. Granted, he could be a bit arrogant, but, an important distinction, he was never condescending. He never spoke down to us. In reading his text, I felt even closer to him. I resolved not to tell anyone about it. Irma would no doubt not have been surprised or even shocked, but it would not have pleased her. As for everyone else, always so prompt to judge . . . 'We judge when we have things to hide. Or when we regret not having any!' Gigi once told me.

It was agreed that I could use the flat as long as I wanted. In any case, until I graduated from medical school. Irma didn't intend to sell it. So I settled in. And I started to look in Gigi's computer, in search of the mysterious Clara. Since he didn't have a password, it was easy to get into his email. But I searched in vain, because I could find no trace of that woman. I was getting more and more frustrated. In the end, I decided to call a friend who knew a girl whose fiancé worked as a hacker for military intelligence (two words which, when placed alongside each other, always made Gigi smile). The guy came over. And he quickly discovered another email account with several email addresses, one of which—gigi.maturelove@ alice.it—was the right one.

Everything was there. Stripped bare. Literally.

There was even a selfie in which the two of them are on a beach, leaning against a rock, naked. I laughed. Until I realized that I knew the place. It was on our island, Sardinia. Had he taken her to our vacation house? A sacrilege. I didn't know what to think. I continued to read. All night long. It was her. In one of her emails, she said she had a new mobile phone and gave him the new number, which I wrote down. It's a good thing I did, because a few days later, their entire correspondence had disappeared. She had deleted it.

And I now understood what the manuscript was. It was a book they had decided to write together. Just for fun. To document their love for each other. For themselves. Not for public consumption (though, on that subject, they kept changing their minds). In any case, they had made an agreement. He would send her his part when he completed it. She would read it carefully to take out anything that might betray them. Then she would 'respond' by delivering her own version of their story.

I wondered if she would still be interested in doing it. Unlike Gigi, I spoke French. I called her.

'You weren't quick enough . . . not quick enough to destroy the emails.'

There was a long silence.

'My name is Elvira. I'm his daughter. I loved him, too. I'd like to give you something.'

'Send it to me by email. It's his manuscript, isn't it?'

Her voice was firm but soft. It moved me.

'I'd like to meet you, talk to you. A half hour, no more. I can catch a plane tomorrow. Meet you wherever you'd like. Please . . .'

She was still in Rome. She had attended the funeral and kept delaying her return to Brussels. Yes, she was Belgian. So what? She didn't want to come to the flat, so we decided to meet at Titti's. It was still early. Via Tacchini. The restaurant was empty. We were given Gigi's usual table in a corner of the small courtyard. A fragrant breeze floated in the air. Jasmine and overripe peaches.

The last time I had been there was for Gigi's seventieth birthday. Clara was curious, but no more than that. She asked me very few questions. None about me or Irma. I imagine that she already knew everything. Gigi must have told her everything. We spent a few hours together. It was I who questioned her. I tried to convince her. Would she do it? Would she fulfil her side of the agreement? I saw her smile for the first time.

'First, I need to read what he wrote again. Then I'll decide.'

I handed her the manuscript with her corrections. And a USB drive. I asked her again if she wanted to come with me to the flat. Then I realized there were tears in her eyes. It looked like she was trembling.

'Not now, no. Not now . . . Soon, perhaps.'

I touched her hand.

'I dreamt of him last night. After reading his text. In my dream he looked happy. His eyes were laughing. He talked. He said something like, "—so, my desire to leave the imprint of my genius on the world . . . that desire has vanished . . . like myself . . . " I don't remember what happened next, but there was something in his voice that was clear and irrefutable.'

She laughed.

'Clear and irrefutable. Yes, that was him. But as for dreams . . . It's still a bit early for me. I have trouble sleeping.'

'Maybe reading this will help?'

She laughed again.

'Why? Is it boring?'

I must have blushed a little.

'Not at all, I just wanted to say . . . If you read it in bed, you might feel his presence. Did it ever happen that you cried together?'

She didn't seem to find the question strange. On the contrary, she told me how they communicated their missing each other. When they couldn't be together they would send text messages to describe the intensity: YLH (yearning level high, missing strong), YLVH (very high) or YLVVH (unbearable).

'Did you write in English?'

'Apart from Italian, that was the only language your father knew. As for myself, I am sometimes, how do you say, limited in your language, we would go from one to the other, we mixed the two . . .'

'And what happened in the case of YLVVH?'

'It was the signal that we had to see each other. Usually, we were able to make it happen.'

She kissed me on the cheeks and then left. I sat at the table for a moment, thinking about the two of them.

Love. Of course, love was important to me, too. But I had the impression . . . How can I put it? You meet, you meld together, you share everything, smells in bed, dreams of the future, music, films, and then, one day, you don't know each other any more. Desire is gone, you get annoyed . . . Anyway, that's what had happened to me not so long ago. But maybe it was something else? *L'amore giovane*? The opposite of the *mature love* of their email addresses? Do emotions ripen, too? Maybe the love I had tasted was too green. Still too young, as they say of wine. Maybe I had only felt young feelings and resentment, young jealousy, young hatred, young indifference. And also the young need to quickly forget a relationship whose meaning was ultimately as feeble as its duration.

He and Clara had been lucky. They had had something infinitely more precious. In any case, that's what I felt when I read Gigi's journal.

Gigi

What is happening to me? I feel younger. I'm sleeping . . . I'm sleeping so well that I'm dreaming of my childhood. It's summer. I'm spending the night under the stars, as I used to do in Sardinia. A smell of burnt milk comes over me. I recognize it. It's the smell of *budino alla mandorla*, the almond pudding that my mother used to make on vacation. Or in Rome on Sunday morning.

The smells of Sunday morning woke me up. Clara was still sleeping in my arms. I kissed her eyelids. She smiled. Without opening her eyes. I remember how, at the beginning of our relationship, she would ask me why. Why I loved her. 'Give me ten good reasons.'

One day I had had enough. I wrote her a poem. It worked very well. Clara never again asked me for reasons. Later, she explained that earlier she wasn't sure she could trust me. She needed reassurance.

She was sleeping. I caressed her back. She didn't move. The second time we made love we were in Berlin, in a hotel.

It seems so long ago now. Four years and four months. The moon was waning and we were listening to a Beethoven sonata. In the *allegro assai*, we realized that the dance of our bodies matched the tempo of the movement, as in a game. After a while, we anticipated it. A race against Ludwig. He won . . . In the *allegro ma non troppo* . . . we had to wait for the *presto*, anticipating the climax. In the final movement, we fell asleep. The next day, Clara wanted to listen to the sonata again. Had Beethoven composed it in complete emotional turmoil? I didn't know, but I said yes, I was sure.

That day, we didn't get out of bed, we watched Antonioni films all day.

'Have you seen *L'Eclisse*? No? . . . ah . . . you'll see how Antonioni shows Rome in the Fifties. In full consumer boom. A world where the power of money—its power to shatter lives—is seen everywhere.'

I explained to Clara why the guy is a genius.

'Look how he films the stock market. A cleverly orchestrated ballet. A choreography. He makes it the last "alive" place when, everywhere else, emotions are unravelling, couples are falling apart.'

In the middle of the film, Monica Vitti confesses to Alain Delon: 'I wish I had never loved you, or that I had loved you much more.' Clara tickles me. What would be my answer if she said that to me? I paused the film. And answered her in actions, like a good southern Italian. Then we finished watching the movie.

Hotels are our refuges. We choose luxurious and cosy ones. But the clandestine lovers we had become must always be on their guard. In Clara's native country, in particular. In Brussels, Bruges, her family, her in-laws, her friends are everywhere. Caution. Even if it's annoying not to be able to go out and hold hands, you have to be careful. It's bearable if the time between two meetings isn't too long. Otherwise, YLVVH. Missing becomes intolerable, as in any love story. There is no age limit for missing someone. The feeling of missing doesn't care. It doesn't care about when we were born.

I continued caressing her. From the neck to her lower back. I still can't believe that this woman whom I met four years, four months and three days ago, could have become the throbbing heart of my existence. She turned over. Her face was completely relaxed. Her eyes were closed. A happy smile lit up her face. We made love. Then I put my head on her chest and fell asleep.

Sometimes we can't talk to each other. When she's on vacation with her family, or I with mine. Those are times of utter torture. At first, when our love was still growing day by day, the only thing we wanted was peace. We had become blind to the world outside. One day, on an almost deserted beach in Greece—there had been only three or four other people there—she put her large linen scarf over our heads so we couldn't see anyone. The idea that the others could still see us didn't bother my Belgian ostrich. On the contrary, it made her laugh.

Like on the Greek beach, she then put the sheet over our heads. I was in her, but she asked me not to move. She wanted to talk. Clara and I talk a lot. When it isn't she, it's I who start. We cover all subjects. As all lovers do, we always go back to origins. Our first meeting. Games, tenderness. We pretend to argue over which one fell in love first. And where. Places are important in these reconstructions. One name and ten emotions come back.

'What about your first love?' Clara asked.

'I can't remember.'

'You can't remember?'

'No.'

She obviously didn't believe it.

'Come on, that's not possible. You have to remember. You're not senile. Make an effort . . . '

'I assure you. It's what is sometimes called priapic love. Not that I'm comparing myself to Priapus, but you understand what that means . . . animal friction of the mucous membranes. Love without emotion, overdetermined by the technical performance, and which leaves almost no memory.'

She insisted. Moved away. Rolled me onto my back and straddled my stomach. She immobilized my hands in a position that prevented caresses or diversions.

'*Try harder* . . . '

I laughed.

'I assure you . . . I remember the girl I was in love with when I was eleven. I remember my mother shrieking in fear when she intercepted our secret correspondence. I remember that her shouting seemed completely hypocritical because she, my mother, had left home when she wasn't even eighteen to run away with my father. I remember the first woman who seduced me and introduced me to orgasms when I was only fifteen (but I don't remember how I could have escaped my mother's vigilance to do it. Maybe she was busy pleasing someone, too?). I remember the man who often came to the house and didn't hide his 'admiration' for her. I remember that it obviously pleased my mother, even if she tried hard not to show anything. I remember that I wanted my mother to remarry. To be at peace. But when she finally did get married, to a vaguely degenerate Englishman who wrote spy novels, I had already left the family nest. You see, I remember all that, but . . . '

'—But?'

'Yes, of course, I also remember the Sixties and Seventies . . . when everything merged together, ideas of love, revolution, liberation . . . When men and women thought we were able to abolish bourgeois emotions for ever. And we paraded that with banners: *No more jealousy*! *Marriage equals prison*! Or *Long Live the clitoris*! That made my mother laugh. "They'll get over it," she would say.'

My parents often came up in our conversations. I told Clara how they had met, in 1942, in the anti-Fascist resistance. Just before Stalingrad, two years before I was born. What they called Resistance was in fact the flipside of a hideous civil war that divided Italy in two approximately equal parties. When it became obvious that the Allies were going to win, loads of careerists discreetly changed camps to join *i partigiani*. My father was killed by a group of fascists, not far from Turin, in March 1945. That week, the week of his death, he had come to visit us, at home. I remember a photo of the three of us together. I'm playing with his beard, he's smiling. For years, I kept that photo with me. But one of my granddaughters, Giulietta, liked it so much that I gave it to her. It was my only souvenir of him.

My grandmother had told me stories about him. It was in Sassari. I stayed with her when my parents were off fighting. Today, when I think about it, I can't shake the idea that my father's death is veiled in mystery. Killed, yes. But by whom? Fascists? Or some individual taking advantage of the chaos to settle some score? My mother never told me anything. But the vehemence with which she defended her version, the official version, always seems suspicious to me. I tried to get close to the truth. All my attempts ended in her stonewalling. I dropped it. Long after my father's death, she took the English lover. He had fought with the *partigiani*, too. I didn't hate him, because he had never attempted to replace my father. Which didn't prevent me from sometimes wondering if he might have killed him . . . accidentally.

My two parents had been active in the PCI. A portrait of Gramsci that had belonged to them was stuck up above my desk. When the Soviet tanks entered Prague, in the summer of 1968, my mother left the Party with the Manifesto Group. But in her opinion, those people were still too attached to Togliatti. My mother said that if Antonio Gramsci had survived the war, the PCI would have come out of it stronger. In truth, she said that because she was sentimental. If Gramsci had escaped Mussolini's prisons, he would have certainly had the same fate that Stalin had reserved for all great foreign communists, and we would have found ourselves with Togliatti in any event. Gramsci, that amazing thinker, was cursed. They succeeded in 'preventing his brain from functioning'. But what he left behind him—which was published after his death—is *un tesoro*, a goldmine.

After my father's death, my mother started writing fiction. She became one of the best Italian women novelists—even if no one here, in my opinion, surpasses the great Sicilians that my friend Vincenzo had introduced me to one day: Federico De Roberto, the prince of Lampedusa, Sciascia . . . and my mother agreed: 'We can't all live on Olympus.' When she died, she bequeathed everything to me. Her royalties financed my first film. Her Englishman had died a few years before her, leaving us a little cottage in Lewes, in Sussex. Since we rarely went there, I sold it without regret. The money allowed me to buy a little fisherman's house in my secret cove on the coast of Sardinia.

I was telling all of this to the woman who was sitting on top of me. Like a child, I told her that I missed my mother. She was more than a mother, she was a friend, a confidante. It was she who, when I was a teenager, consoled my first broken heart. Clara took me in her arms and hugged me tightly. 'One is never too old to be a child,' she said. Then she switched gears, going back in time. To the feminist banners of the Sixties:

'This clitoris business . . . it's utterly commonplace these days . . . '

'Maybe, but jealousy is always a hot topic . . . '

And then we set off on a new subject, jealousy, that secret emotion, almost shameful, but so terribly tenacious. Jealousy and its destructive hold over our lives. In this regard, I agree that even *mature lovers* aren't exempt from it.

'Really?' she said, giving me an inquisitive look.

I admitted that a sort of jealousy started to slither in when I imagined her in the arms of her legitimate partner. Nothing violent. Nothing that tormented me. But, how could I put it . . . A permanent smell of sour vinegar.

I explained that, for us men, the feeling probably went back to the distant days of feudalism. When the woman was part of the goods of the seigniory. Of its mode of production. Originally, I'm a historian who makes films, but I've never given up my first passion. We don't remake ourselves entirely . . .

'Do you know that, on our continent, the chastity belt was invented by the first Christians before it was used by the knights and lords of the Middle Ages? Their aim was simple: to protect their "property" while they went off to war, lock up the woman's genitals and take away the key—I'm talking about the real key, not metaphorically about the male sex organ . . . '

Clara pretended to sigh.

'Of course, Gigi, everyone knows that.'

'When they arrived in the Holy Land, the crusaders found men and women who covered their heads for protection from the sun, but who would never have dreamt of locking up women's genitals in belts!'

'Do you really think that those women were completely faithful?'

'No, of course not. To each poison its antidote. European locksmiths were perfectly capable of producing duplicate keys if someone was willing to pay for them . . . Let's not forget that many of those women tended to the family domain while their husbands were away. So, if they could manage entire estates alone, they were certainly capable of taking care of their own body. Which they often did. And with the most varied of lovers. You might say that, up to a recent date, the bourgeoisie adapted that system, but it didn't fundamentally change it.'

'I agree, but why are you lecturing me all of a sudden?'

'You're right, I didn't intend to talk about that "jealousy of ownership". But about the other . . . the one with which we're all too familiar. The one that claims to protect what is most intimate, the heart, the mind, memories. That jealousy is connected to love like an umbilical cord.'

I began to tell Clara about certain episodes in my past. As if I were lifting the cover off of 'my' women at the time. The unwashed cover from the flat in Rome where I lived with two friends, when we were all at La Sapienza, in the Sixties. I try not to think about them. One was killed by the police. The other had switched sides. De Berlinguer fired Berlusconi after a detour through the socialist Nenni. Today, that bastard is a multimillionaire. Life in hell suits him. Every year he sends me a holiday card. But he shouldn't have any illusions: card or no card, I will not be going to his funeral.

In any case, as regards women, of course I remember them. Most of them, by the way, remained friends. But love came only later. And not in Rome. In Turin.

At that moment, my gaze was fixed on Clara. But the exquisite creature that I was holding in my arms suddenly seemed less interested in what I was telling her. Too bad—I continued to the end of the story. So, in Turin. Today, Irma the Turinese is still my wife. Professor of literature at the University of Turin and the author of three books, one of which, on Boccaccio and Dante, is excellent—I can say that, because I am her toughest critic.

We have two children. One is the delightful Elvira who is studying medicine and who is the proverbial apple of my eye. So I guess I can say my life is *settled*. Too much so, perhaps. As for passion . . . that is, indeed, where the difficulty lies. Each of us has our routines. Common friends, the same political ideas. I like to cook, swim, walk, but as for the rest . . . Anyway, what's the use of worrying about it? As a Neapolitan proverb goes, *there's no need to shake the old tree if no breath of wind is disturbing the leaves*.

Clara stared at me, silent.

'It was before you,' I told her.

It was before Clara, and I had ended up resolving myself to my lot. The way one resolves oneself to the normal course of things. Well, maybe.

I had just wrapped up a new film. An important milestone in my work which had gone completely unnoticed by the critics. From semi-surrealism to neo-neorealism, I had arrived at biopics. Somewhat along the lines of the ones that Rossellini did right after the war. Unconsciously, I probably was telling myself that, by paying tribute to him in this way, I would perhaps find a woman like Anna Magnani or Ingrid Bergman, both of whom were his wives. Or Marlene Dietrich, one of his many mistresses. In any case, even in my wildest fantasies I would have never imagined him with Sonali Dasgupta, that young, twenty-seven-year-old beauty he met while filming in India, and for whom Rossellini abandoned his wonderful Swedish wife. Poor Sonali. And she was happily married. But she hadn't been able to resist. Enflamed by the fire lit by my compatriot, she left her husband, a talented documentarian, a friend of Satyajit Ray. It was a huge scandal in India. The prime minister at the time, Nehru, offered to help the couple. Rossellini brought Dasgupta back to Rome, where he broke up with her in a . . . shall we say, casual way. By telling a painter friend, Guttuso, that the voracious beast that was his virile member demanded variety. There was a rumour that the great seducer even asked the artist to paint the beast in colour. It was also said that Guttuso, usually happy to go along with that sort of erotic joke, had refused. *Ci sono limiti all'amicizia.*

Sonali's family knew the writer Rabindranath Tagore well. When they were still together, Sonali took Rossellini to the Taj Mahal. There, she read out loud to him the verses of Tagore. A poem of command that Rossellini immediately hated. Was it at that moment that he understood he had made a mistake? A mistake about Sonali? He at least was honest enough to tell her he didn't like Tagore. Not that Tagore. What Rossellini didn't tell her was that he had wanted to go to Agra to com-memorate a wedding anniversary that he had once celebrated there with Anna Magnani. But I sensed that, once again, my interest in film history was leading me astray. We got back to my film—the one Rossellini should have done, but which he never did.

My grandparents were Sardinian. In 1906, they had immi-grated to Turin. A bit later, they were joined by the son of their former neighbours in Sardinia. Tonio. That was his name. My grandmother even called him 'our Tonio'. Until the day when, in the Thirties, a fascist heard her, walked up to her, and cru-elly pinched her breast. That would teach her to talk tenderly about that red bastard, that Gramsci who was fortunately rot-ting in Mussolini's prisons.

Il Duce. No one dares attack him, ever since he has returned to fashion. Since he's living again, in a sense. Whereas Gramsci is indeed dead . . . I've never forgotten that episode. It was what made me want to make a film about him. Gramsci, his life, his work. My wife claims it's only an excuse to spend some time relaxing in Sardinia. That I was never really inter-ested in his books. She's not entirely wrong. However, I strug-gled to obtain whatever funding I could for the film, but I persisted in wanting to do it. Around me, in Italy, people shrugged. What's the point? 'Why not leave Gramsci's memory to fade in the prison where he indeed deserved to be thrown?' A journalist said to me during a premiere at the Nuovo Sacher in Trastevere. That idiot was already completely soused. I thought that a few more drops wouldn't hurt him, and I poured my glass of red wine on his shiny skull. Then I watched the wine drip drop by drop down his fat, red cheeks, then onto his beige suit. He grabbed a cheese knife from the buffet table. Pathetic. His wife held him back. Even more pathetic. And from that moment the idea for the film became very enticing to me.

I immersed myself in Gramsci. Seriously, meticulously. I read everything. And, even though his ideas seem outdated today, I fell in love. Gramsci opened my eyes to the Italian shipwreck, its foundering culture, its corrupt politicians, everything *beyond repair*. He tells how the monster of Emilia-Romagna ensured at the time that he would be seen as the personification of Hope. The hope, shining new, of an unmoored Italy.

You might ask, why go back to that? Stir up that past once again? We can live without getting involved in all that again, can't we? Of course we can. Live in a comfortable house, drink good coffee, eat organic, see friends and forget what my father-in-law called *the big picture*. That's what people do, in general. As for me, I prefer another sort of failure. That's why I plunged into that film.

One day, my publicist called. *Gramsci* had just been released in Anvers. And Clara Magnani, the great Belgian critic—the one who hosted the best cultural programme on the radio—wanted to interview me. A long, one-on-one interview. Magnani. Clara Magnani. That name rang a bell. I googled her. Yes, it was really she. We had met briefly at a film festival, in Greece, a few years earlier. She hadn't said a lot, but she hadn't made an unfavourable impression on me. Of course, we talked about films. I pointed out to her that the young Belgian cinema was far superior to what was being done in France, and she had smiled.

'I hope you're not saying that just because I'm Belgian . . . '

Oh, no. That wasn't my style. My friends knew that well. I'm usually pretty critical. Some of them even accuse me of being overly critical. A grudge against the world . . . That's clearly not the case. On the other hand, I have nothing but the greatest contempt for the political and cultural elite who are governing us. That makes me poor company at 'politically correct' dinners. I mentioned three young Belgian filmmakers to Clara Magnani. She nodded in agreement. She seemed vaguely distracted that evening, in Greece, and didn't want to linger after dinner. When I got up to say goodbye, I noticed she was almost as tall as I. She was wearing slacks and sneakers. Reddish-brown hair, she looked Flemish, but no, she was indeed Walloon. I remember asking myself—Lord knows how the idea came to me—what size her feet were and if she could fit in my shoes.

But let's get back to Rome, where I spend every winter. Not in the stifling heart of the city, where pilgrims and tourists scuttle around, but in the Parioli quarter. The flat belonged to my mother. Fortunately, when she died, I didn't have to buy any shares from my brothers and sisters—I don't have any. One advantage of being an only child . . . That is where Clara Magnani showed up to interview me. At the end of September, in the early afternoon. There were still flowers on my mother's terrace. Overripe lemons, but perfect for cooking. On the wall, the bougainvillea and the jasmine were entwined. That day, the sky was cloudless. Pale blue. Like her jeans. Clara was wearing a white blouse, the sleeves rolled up to her elbows. Her green eyes blended in with the foliage. I noticed their velvety texture. And how they seemed to change. Lively, sparkling, then suddenly sad. I think it's that sadness that first intrigued me. The woman seemed fragile and passionate to me. Or maybe the opposite.

'Fantastic terrace,' she said.

Everyone said that. We sat in the kitchen. I offered her tea, coffee, fresh apricot juice, homemade lemonade, wine . . . She asked for water. A salad? No, she didn't have a lot of time. Her two sons—twins—were at the hotel, near the Piazza del Popolo. They were probably getting bored. I suggested she call them. They could join us for lunch. She seemed surprised. It wasn't possible. She had convinced them to go with her that evening to the Teatro dell'Opera. Verdi. *Un ballo in Maschera* . . . And so she needed to spend the afternoon with them. Otherwise, they might disappear or change their minds.

My children never went to the opera or to any classical concert with me. I was impressed. A good mother and a pretty woman . . . How old could she be? Almost forty, more or less? Or was it a false impression due to Advanced Night Repair 1 (I, myself, use 2). Her children had just graduated from college. Later, I learnt that she was over forty-five. Exactly forty-six. *Niente male*. Not bad. Our ages weren't that far apart. But just the fact that I was wondering betrayed . . . What? That I was on the defensive? As if I was being asked to prove my virility?

She had prepared the interview well. She wasn't just relying on articles and reviews. She had even seen the film, which wasn't always the case with every journalist. Granted, she had never read Gramsci, but she knew who he was—that was something these days. Unless she had read the details of his entry on Wikipedia? Yes, she told me frankly. And the fact that she wasn't attempting to hide it completely disarmed me. Since I don't speak French, we began the interview in Italian. From time to time, we moved to English, and for the first time, I was very grateful to my mother's British lover.

'Were you really faithful to the facts? Is it true that malnutrition had deformed Gramsci's spine so that his mother, ignoring her son's protesting, hung him regularly from the ceiling beams to "straighten him out"? That is one of the most striking scenes in the film. I wondered . . . Was it true, or did you embellish it?'

'Not at all, all of that really happened. Specialists are aware. But what I did make up, on the other hand, is Gramsci's conversation in bed with his lover.'

'Hmmm . . . Not the best scene in the film . . . '

I laughed.

'What is the best, then?'

'The debate in the Parliament. When Gramsci addresses Mussolini. It's great. And the question Mussolini asks in return is far from stupid. You were right not to cut it . . . '

'Cut it? How could I have? It was the great paradox all the communists at that time were confronted with. They fought for the defence of unions, supported opposition parties, fought against the suppression of some newspapers, but, as far as the Soviet Union went, they did exactly the opposite.

Only because the same measures, over there, were taken by their comrades . . . Oh, history! Oh, sadness!' I sighed.

I added a bit to impress her. Usually, interviews quickly bored me. Selling myself always seemed so debasing. Ah, a world without (self-) promotion! The questions are always the same. The answers, too. So I tune out. I go on automatic pilot. Until . . . *è finita la commedia*.

With her, it was different. I would have been happy for it to go on indefinitely. But she was a professional. She had scheduled an hour, no more. That's how she worked at the radio station. An important guest every week. Over time, it probably became tiresome for her, too. She stood up, verified that her recorder had worked. Then she smiled. Rather, her lips smiled. Because her eyes weren't smiling.

After she thanked me, she swallowed a final mouthful of water, picked up her scarf that was hanging on the back of a chair, and held out her hand. To my great surprise—but I think to hers, too—I heard myself offer to take her back to her hotel. She hesitated. I wanted to tell her something funny. Something like: 'Never fear, Madame, I am no more dangerous than your husband.' But would she have laughed? I babbled something. I was going in that direction in any case. To the dentist . . . In the car, I wondered what had come over me. It had all been so impulsive. We didn't talk a lot. I said two or three innocuous things about the Villa Borghese. Delivered a few platitudes that I came up with. Once again, she smiled. But always the same polite smile, the one on her lips, but not in her eyes.

I dropped her off near her hotel, Piazza del Popolo. We said goodbye in an entirely formal way. Then I went home, thinking about her all the way. My instinct . . . My instinct told me that there was something else behind her self-assurance. My first impression returned. Passionate and fragile. That's what she was. In any case, it's what her eyes told me about her.

No sooner had I arrived home than I was seized by an irresistible desire to rush to the Teatro dell'Opera. *Un ballo in maschera* is not my favourite piece. Far from it. But that wasn't important. I tried to reason with myself. Wouldn't she be with her children? The idea was outrageous. What had come over me? Get a grip, I told myself. Be dignified. At your age, one must advance towards the end in the most elegant way possible. However, I was assailed by the thoughts of a teenager. As if my emotional mind was commanding my body to awaken. To have an adventure. While another part of myself was telling me to calm down. *Basta così*. It was time to get back to work.

I dove back into my reading. Neorealism in post-war Italian cinema. That was the theme of the lecture I was giving at the Djakarta Film Festival in two weeks. Visconti, De Sica, Rossellini, Rosi; the explosive irruption of Fellini; and finally, a few years later, the return of realism with Pontecorvo, whose masterpiece on the Algerian war, *La Battaglia di Algeri*, had been quickly censured by the French authorities.

I had all the DVDs in a stack on my desk. In principle, nothing should have been more pleasant than the prospect of watching them comfortably in the coming ten days—something I had begun to do. But Clara's face kept coming back.

Superimposing itself on the moving images. Forcing me to hit 'pause' to think about her. The feeling that arose in me was as unexpected as it was irrational, but it was far from disagreeable. As if an intimate volcano, lying dormant for ages, was once again beginning to slowly, emotionally, erupt. Was it possible that it was still possible? I hadn't experienced that state for a very long time. Since my affair with . . .—but I preferred not to think about that episode that had damaged my marriage and upset my children. At that time, I had sworn to myself that something like that would never happen again. I had thrown buckets of cold water on any embers that still remained.

Life had gradually gone back to normal. But never as it had been before. The children proved to be the most resilient. Irma and I . . . How can I put it? From that time, we each lived in our own space. We remained close and good friends, but the trust had been destroyed. We never talked to each other again in the same way. At that time, I had done three films. One had been relatively more successful than the other two. As for Irma, probably inspired by my mother's experience, she threw herself entirely into a historiographical study of the role of women in the Italian Resistance. *La storia quotidiana delle donne nell'antifascismo.*

And now? What was happening to me? I scarcely knew this Mme Magnani, and it was highly unlikely that we would have an opportunity to meet again. Unless? Hadn't she pointed out that she would contact me in the event that she needed more details or additional material? We could then talk on Skype and . . . No. The battle between the me who hoped and the one who attempted to reason with me flared up again. Come on. Enough. I sat down in front of *Il gattopardo*. It was clear, obviously, that I had been wrong. This film defied all conventions. It also showed that the principle according to which no great novel leads to a great film, in particular with Hollywood actors, was false. I had been wrong in holding that opinion for so long. I should have watched it again. Watched it again sooner. Each scene is so artistically constructed that the whole is a delight. For two hundred and five minutes, Claudia Cardinale pushed aside the Lady from the Brabant. Clara, I know her, wouldn't have liked to read that. Excluded from my thoughts? Even at that stage in our relationship, the idea would have horrified her. She was so afraid of an adventure without a future.

That evening, I grabbed my notebook and went out for a walk. The air was warm. The sky streaked with red. For dinner, I went to Titti's, where they serve ravioli, *madre di Dio*, like nowhere else in Rome. And they're only ten minutes from where I live. Titti, where I've eaten since forever. It's one of the rare, still civilized, spots in the pseudo-eternal city. I keep not my napkin ring, but my bottle of wine there. While dining, I drink a glass or two. Then they hold on to it for me until the next time.

And so that evening, I was taking notes while enjoying a Sassicaia 2007. I'm not saying that *per darmi arie*, as Clara would say—she adored that expression, 'to put on airs', which in Italian quite simply means 'show off'—but to point out the grand cru from Tuscany for the true oenophiles. In this case, but how could it have been otherwise, the bottle had been given to me by someone in his nineties, a very refined and cultivated historian, though deeply conservative, who lived in Venice part of the year, had known Thomas Mann, and was in love with me. The guy knew that he was barking up the wrong tree, but he enjoyed my company. He had one of the most beautiful libraries in Venice, not to mention his wine cellar. Once, I filmed a scene in his sitting room. A feature film whose screenplay I had not written, and which is by far my worst film. But the Rai 3 had found it amusing and it was a hit. Enough, in any case, to wipe out my debts.

When I was about to leave Titti's that evening, I glanced at my notebook. Everything I had scribbled in it was summed up by this: *Magna, Magnani, Magnanima.* And this stupid question: *Does she have a magnanimous lover?* That evening, my contribution to neorealism stopped there.

Two weeks later, I was in Djakarta. My lecture was well received. I had met a group of young writers and directors obsessed with the history of Indonesia, in particular with the massacres of 1965. One of them, a poet, invited me to spend a few days at his villa in Bali. Why not? I had never been to that island. I was disappointed. The only worthwhile thing about the trip was, again, connected to Clara. I had received an email: *Where are you? I need a few more details about Gramsci. We will also need a few voice-offs and archive images for our Internet site. Will that be possible?*

I can still see myself the next day, laughing to myself at breakfast. I had just read the headlines of the *Bali Times,* which included this edifying story that I immediately told her about in an email.

'*Cow Sex Returns to Bali*—today's headline in the Indonesian newspaper. *The daughter of a farmer—rather of the owner of a cow—found her husband (and the father of their three children) pleasuring himself with the cow.* Then there's the opinion of a psychiatrist, Luth Keti Suryani, on the magnetism exercised over some humans by what he calls *temptress bovines.* What is saddest about this affair, he adds, is that the *defiled cow* had to be slaughtered. Mr Suryani continues: *The man—lover of bovines—remembers the precise moment when he penetrated the animal. "It was as if I were floating in another dimension. Before me was a young girl . . . or in any case, a being that appeared to be a young girl and who was the very essence of femininity. She came up to me and seduced me . . ."* In the original version, the psychiatrist concluded in these terms: *From a modern health perspective, we must examine the possibility that the person who commits such an action may have mental problems.*'

I also gave Clara this important additional information. A few months earlier, there had been a similar case involving a young, eighteen-year-old man, the *Bali Times* pointed out. That time, they had forced the man to marry the cow. *On behalf of the cow, some people attempted to protest against the forced marriage. But to no avail, and the cow was drowned after the wedding.* I ended my email with a note of surprise: *It's curious that in a culture in which cows are sacred, no one mentions the rather 'natural' nature of that transference. I mean, the confusion between the divine object and the love object . . .*

Clara responded immediately. *I'm reading this at the office and you're making me laugh. But why in the world would you share such a crazy story with me? Does it in fact reveal your own fantasies? . . .*

That's how our friendship began. Lightly on her side. Much less so on mine. But playful on both our sides. She had written a glowing review of the film, and I was invited to Brussels to give a lecture after a filming. Then, there was a dinner at her house. I met her husband there, her twins, and two other brilliant critics. I remember clearly what she was wearing that evening. A low-cut red dress that highlighted her neck and her shoulders, and just hinted at the tops of her breasts. A fabulous chest, that's what I thought. She was wearing an antique gold necklace from Central Africa. Stolen by one of her ancestors in colonial times? Not at all. Her sister, she told me, was an anthropologist, a specialist in matriarchal traditions in the Niger Valley. She had brought it back from Mali. I also remember how she had fixed her hair. It was pulled up in a bun, and gave her a serious and solemn air. The meal, the wine, everything was good. But, given the way she accepted the compliments, I understood that she hadn't done anything herself.

Her husband, Hieronymus Vercammen, a physics professor, was at the height of his career, and had a post at Princeton. Often mentioned for a Nobel Prize, he was the official science advisor to the Belgian government. Involved in many European projects, including the surveillance programme for Iranian nuclear reactors. Everyone called him Ron. The Americans had given him that nickname, and it had stuck. In his fifties, well-dressed, that evening he was wearing an elegant suit, large enough to hide his potbelly. He was witty, and laughed a lot, but too loudly and too frequently for my taste. Was it an authentic laugh, or forced? Probably a bit of both. A laugh that wanted to attract attention. Ron seemed to be a good man. And yet, I didn't feel the least contrition at the idea of having fallen madly in love with his wife. In any event, what can you do in such a case? In the case of love? Nip all feeling in the bud? Accept a sort of inner death? Since I had met Clara, I wasn't—was no longer—at all ready for that.

Her children seemed well behaved and intelligent. Was it my imagination? I had the impression that one of her sons was observing the guests. There was some cynicism and a bit of malice in his eye. Was he inventing a mocking nickname for each guest with which he would regale the family after dinner? The idea was funny, and I liked thinking about it.

That evening, I made a huge effort not to look at Clara, who was also ignoring me. She had put me beside an old lady, who seemed to be celebrating her eightieth birthday, and a musician who was known locally. With Ron sitting opposite me, I was being punished. Had she found my Balinese humour offensive? I shouldn't have joked about bovine love . . . and yet.

If only she could have known what I was feeling. As I was leaving, I whispered in her ear:

'The other day, you know, I almost followed you to the Teatro dell'Opera. In Rome . . .'

She seemed stupefied, ignored what I said, and held out her hand in quasi-indifference.

Back in Rome, I can see myself pacing back and forth in my flat. I told myself that in the past, people thought a lot more before sending a love letter. There were many considerations to take into account. Where to send it, for example—the house was impossible, but was the workplace safe enough? Should it be mailed, or delivered directly to the recipient? By eliminating those sorts of questions, the internet made men bolder. Write, send, and the one you're lusting after is already reading what you wrote. As a subject line I had chosen: *Innamoramento*. A magnificent word that designates the moment when you fall in love, and for which there is no equivalent in other languages. Not in English, or in the Scandinavian languages. Not even, I was told, in a language like French, which has such a rich vocabulary for love.

Thank you for the excellent dinner. I was delighted to sit opposite your husband. A charming and intelligent man. But you were sitting as far from me as possible. Was that intentional? Or meant to make you even more irresistible? Dear Clara, let's get away for a few days to talk about our future. Anywhere far from Brussels and Rome. Germany? Berlin, Munich? Do you have a personal email address? I wouldn't want our exchanges to become the laughing stock of your colleagues in the RTBF lunchroom. I await your response with hope and impatience.

Giangiacomo G.

Her response was as quick as it was to the point.

> I'm glad that you liked the dinner. And liked my husband. I like him, too. And I have no intention of having a tryst with you in Germany. As for emails, I am already overwhelmed, and just the idea of having another email address appals me.
> *Have a good day.*
> Clara

I felt stupid beyond words. How could I have imagined that my feelings were shared? Another typically male assumption, my mother would have scolded. I was mortified. I had to apologize. *Have a good day* was written in English, which exasperated me. Why mimic American cashiers? Is that how she saw me? As a consumer?

> I'm very sorry. Because I have fallen madly in love, I immediately imagined that you felt the same. How stupid! How arrogant! If you can forgive me for having been so presumptuous, we might be friends. A light-hearted friendship. And speaking of lightness, know that I completely understand your wish not to have a tryst in Germany. But where, then? Do you have a list of possible countries? I'm joking. In the hope that you'll forgive me. But, despite what you suggest, I will not have a good day.
> GG

That time, there was no response. I hoped she wasn't too angry, but, after a week, I lost hope. She had obviously decided that even an inconsequential friendship wasn't going to happen.

What an idiot I was. I tried to think of other things. I scribbled some notes for a future film on my parents, their circle of friends under Fascism. And the way they had all found each other in the Resistance. But who in this damned country would one day want to finance such a project? Wouldn't it be better to write the screenplay first, even if it meant finding funding in Europe afterwards?

That's where I was in my thinking when I called Béatrice. Bi isn't just my agent. She's a confidante and a friend. I found her in a bad mood when I called. But we agreed to meet at Titti's. When she arrived, she had recovered her smile. And was enthusiastic about my idea. She was sure that we would find funding for the script.

'Are you serious, Bi?'

'Of course, Gigi . . . What's wrong? My neighbour killed my cat yesterday. That's why I'm in a bad mood. What about you? You seem preoccupied. Is something wrong?'

I told her. After a moment, she burst out laughing.

'She rejected you?'

'What do you think?'

'Well . . . What can I tell you? Concentrate on your film. Neither one of us has endless time ahead of us. I have friends in Belgium. Some are very close. Do you want me to ask around about her?'

'What do you mean?'

'Oh, I don't know . . . If I find out that she has a lover, for example, it's best to let it go, don't you think?'

'On the contrary. That would be the most encouraging situation. I would immediately take the bastard's place.'

We laughed.

Bi called me the next day. Clara was very well known and respected. But no rumours about her suggested an extramarital relationship. No, the upshot was that she was distant and cold. Moreover, one of her sources pointed out, she was enthralled with Iceland. She had even confided in a friend that she wanted to learn Icelandic and delve into the culture of the island.

'Maybe she has a true leaning for cold. . .'

'Perhaps.'

I learnt that she had even written a little book on the causes of the collapse of the Icelandic economy. Since the book had been translated into Italian, I immediately ordered a copy. Coincidentally, it arrived the same day I received a letter from her in my mailbox.

> Sorry for not replying earlier. Friendship is a good idea! I'll be in Rome next week. I'm seeing my sister and brother-in-law who is ambassador to Italy. How about a coffee on Piazza Navona? All the best.
>
> Clara

Good heavens. Not the Piazza Navona, which is always lousy with tourists and filled with nuns greedily leering at the Bernini statues. But why not next door, on the Campo de' Fiori, where the statue of Giordano Bruno defies the imbeciles in the Vatican? It was a cool November day. Winter was coming. She arrived wearing a beautiful taupe cashmere coat.

Next to it, my old, moth-eaten black overcoat paled in comparison. We sat down in a corner of a cafe. She was smiling.

'What's new?

'I've fallen in love.'

'Can anything be done about it?'

'No.'

She seemed bothered. I asked her how long she had been married.

'Twenty-four years, and . . . things are good.'

'I can't believe that neither of you . . .'

'We have a rule. The famous—*Don't ask, don't tell.*'

'But . . .'

'There's no "but", dear Sir. Besides, you know, I much prefer admirers over lovers.'

' . . . ?'

'You know the *cicisbeo*? It's in *La Chartreuse de Parme*, you must remember. In French, the word is *sigisbée*. It's a sort of platonic admirer. A man who loves you, courts you, flatters you, and is never discouraged. That's exactly what I'd like. My ego would love that.'

'Ah, but that's completely awful. A cicisbeo is just a gigolo. Granted, platonic. But a gigolo all the same!'

She laughed. This time she really laughed. Spontaneously and sincerely. A wonderful burst of sound coming from deep in her throat. We talked for a half-hour. I suggested we have lunch in the near future. Why not, she said, while stressing the lack of urgency. The conversation moved over various subjects.

To Venice which, in the sixteenth and seventeenth centuries was the most anti-clerical city in Italy—did she know that? Yes. She had even created a fifty-two-minute documentary on that subject. For the radio, of course, not for television, which she hated. We moved on to more important things. I persuaded her of the need to have a personal email address. I could create one for her if she wanted. She said OK, and I did so that very afternoon when I got home. As a password I chose *Innamoramento* for her, an infantile rose-scented code. But love does things like that. Anyone who doubts it should read Stendhal again, in fact. He is the best one on the subject. As for knowing whether that *Innamoramento* was perfect—I'm speaking of password security here—that was another story.

She left the cafe to return to the embassy. She had to get ready for a reception that evening. Right then, I wondered what in life could be more boring than a reception at the Belgian Embassy. I didn't say anything, of course. When she stood up, I asked her if she would button the top button of my old coat and, while she was doing it, I kissed her on the lips. Quickly. Without premeditation. She must have felt how impulsive that kiss was. Because, though shocked, she didn't slap me. But she didn't smile, either, and we parted with a friendly handshake.

Bi called to tell me that someone was interested in my idea on the Resistance—but was I still interested? I walked to her office on Via Pomponio Leto—they serve the best coffee in Rome there—and I told her everything. What did she think? That Clara wasn't as detached as she wanted to seem. That she liked my company, that was clear. But where would it take us? Bi couldn't say anything about that.

'What do you really want from her?' she asked.

'From her? It's her that I want.'

'My dear, Giangiacomo, it's been a long time since I've seen your face so happy,' said Bi. 'But, at our age, you do know how ephemeral these things are.'

'They are at any age.'

'That's true, but—'

'But nothing, Bi. What do you expect to happen? Rather, if anything happens, things are clear. Both of us loves and respects our spouse. Both of us are attached to our children. Neither of us wants to ruin or undo anything. Let's even imagine that my Belgian Beauty develops reciprocal feelings for me, it wouldn't threaten anyone. It's what the English call *mature love*.'

'OK, Giangiacomo, but emotions can lead to . . . hey, don't force me to state the obvious. Just be careful, OK? Mature or not, if this love transcends everything, I don't want to find you like a teenager glued to his phone, waiting for the next message.'

She was silent for a moment, then resumed:

'There's also another danger.'

'What?'

'What if your conversations ended up annoying her? . . . '

I stood up and kissed her on the cheeks.

'Well, if that were to happen, I would leave right away. On tiptoe and gracefully. Could you call me a taxi? I have to go now.'

'We haven't even talked about your new film.'

'We will. As soon as the money is there.'

'That's it?'

'That's it.'

Bi couldn't get a taxi quickly enough, and I ended up walking home. It was much better, anyway. I wanted to be alone to think about Clara in peace. I thought while walking. If he existed—and my instinct told me this was the case—who could her lover be? Someone younger than she? Older? Even older? An Icelandic Jew? A Parisian dandy? A narrow-minded Flemish guy? She didn't want to talk about it in Rome. Would it ever come up again somewhere else? If she were happy, I would indeed have to retreat. In a few months, we would per-haps become friends. *A light-hearted friendship.* Would that be possible? Desirable? Why did all these thoughts churn in my head? In any event, lover or not, it didn't change anything about what I thought of her. But what about her? What was she expecting of me? That I court her, that was clear—a pleas-ant fact, but which had its limits. I had read the stories she had written. Texts published by a small Brussels publisher. The intensity of certain passages led me to believe that a greater proximity was possible. It's strange, the place that this woman had suddenly taken in my life and my thoughts. And almost no one knew about it. Except for her. Was I, and I had to admit it, making a film about myself?

Maybe.

When I got home I looked at my email. On her RTBF email, I let her know that she was now completely free from any control by her company. She had her own email address. We began to correspond, and our friendship developed. One day, she announced that she was going away with her family to Colorado for the Christmas vacation. A friend of Ron's, a colleague at Princeton, had a magnificent house in the mountains there. But without Wi-Fi. Our communications would have to be suspended for two weeks. Torture. I thought that even in the most remote corner of America the smallest burg was connected! I started to write a 'journal of absence'. A journal for the Absent One. I wrote in it every day. She could read it when she got back.

20 December. Can you tell me how I'm going to survive this way for thirteen days? It's too long, my Clara. I'm happy that you liked the Visconti I sent you. I've never read the novel by Gabriele D'Annunzio, but something tells me the film is better. How could that poseur D'Annunzio surpass Visconti? I knew that you'd like *L'innocente*. By the way, did I tell you that, in the past, I did two interviews with the Count—I'm talking about Visconti. Alas, I lost the recordings. What an idiot. The recordings weren't great quality, but even so, I can't forgive myself. Even if I remember rather well what he said . . . Quite a few rants against other directors! What a genius!

21 December. Is there a lot of snow? Is it good? I can see you skiing, your cheeks red with the cold. When I was a child, we often went to the Alps. The villagers tried their best to get me on skis, but I wasn't interested. *Do you agree that all sport is a prison of measured time?*

22 December. Cicisbeo? I think I see the idea. *A man who surrounds a woman with great attention*, according to the dictionary. *Synon. serving knight (s. knight), serving knight (s. knight, mod.; more common)*. '*You're lucky—since she is rather mature—that she will be of absolute discretion. Without that, she would have certainly taken you as a cicisbeo, as they said in my youth, a sort of serving gallant*' (Proust, *Sodom*, 1922, p. 724).

I'll never be a cicisbeo, Clara! Never. Never. Never!

23 December. Until yesterday, I wondered why you never appeared in my dreams. My hypothesis was this: I think about you so much while I am awake that it is impossible for my unconscious to do so, as well. It would be an overdose. But then, this morning, you burst forth. The dream was strange, very strange. I was in Africa. A young woman—how old? Twenty? OK, let's say thirty at the most—was running away. She was obviously trying to get away from someone. I opened the door to my Jeep and offered to take her to the closest city. That's when I saw that her hands were tied together. I stopped the car, cut the rope around her wrists. She began to tell me her story, but I don't remember what she said. In the following scene, that young woman and I—by the way, I must point out that it was a very young me here—that young woman and I, then, were about to make love when I heard your voice. You were pulling on my arm to get me away from her. Then I turned toward you. 'A nightmare?' you asked. You were in the bed next to me. And I woke up.

I tried to interpret it, and then I dropped it. Fundamentally, most dreams are really clichéd. I sometimes wonder if the good Viennese doctor mightn't have made too much of them.

23 December. I'm getting down to work. My new screenplay. If only I had really known my father.

Some old friends from *L'Unità* are coming over for dinner tonight, and my refrigerator is empty. There will be fifteen of us. It's too bad you won't be here. I think I'll make grilled fish with herbs with risotto. If you were a mermaid, I would also grill your tail and I would be the only one to eat it.

24 December. Today, the complete lack of contact is unbearable, my Clara. And what about what comes next? Will it get worse, or lessen? Become prosaic? Reach a plateau? I'm reading *La Conspiration* by Nizan again. I was young when I read it for the first time. I didn't really like it. Today, it's different. I laugh when I see what he called one of his characters, an army officer, Major Sartre. It's too bad Nizan died so young. I'd like to make a film from that book. But maybe it would be better if a French person did it. Although . . . who are the great French filmmakers today? In an hour, I'm leaving for Turin. Join my wife for the holidays.

24 December. It's as long as a day without bread. I'm fed up. With being far from you. In addition, it's cold, and there isn't any coffee in this house. This evening my mother-in-law will be there; she just turned ninety and is going to cook. I'll be content to light the candles. Why in the world must we go through this every year? I'm thinking about the pagans, their feasts and their orgies. I find them a thousand times more inventive in their way of celebrating the winter solstice.

25 December. I was thinking that you didn't have internet access and we wouldn't be able to communicate. I hadn't sent you anything until this morning, and I was proud. And then, this morning, I decided I would send you what I had written. That you would read it when you get back. What a nice surprise to read your email, even if it was wisely disguised under a professional message. But it's too long now, Clara. I want you next to me buttoning the top of my coat. Can we have lunch one day? Can you suggest a date and a place? Your country? Mine? A neutral territory? If that's the case, I'd prefer to avoid Iceland. I've heard that in Reykjavik the only thing to see is the National Museum of Phalluses—I'm not kidding. You can understand that for a man like me, who is attempting an adventure of *mature love*, it's not exactly enticing . . .

26 December. OK, Brussels. It doesn't matter where we have lunch, as long as the wine is good. I'm coming to Brussels to see you, Clara, not to eat. But I will think of a restaurant. There is a place that serves lobster near the Grand-Place . . .

28 December. My screenplay on the Resistance is completely becalmed. I have to respond to an interview, another one, on my mother. The woman and her work. It's not easy. I don't want her unpleasant side to be revealed in public.

30 December. I wonder if you're thinking about me.

31 December. You must be dancing with all the beautiful people . . . Clara, can you explain to me why my love for you isn't fading, isn't weakening, isn't softening? Why it isn't reaching a 'plateau'?

I found these lines by an Arab poet whom I like a lot—he's dead—and had written this to his beloved when he was in Rome on a New Year's Eve:

> *To my beloved, on New Year's Eve*
> *I love you*
> *It has nothing to do*
> *With water or wind*
> *Or with the movement of the tides*
> *Or solar eclipses*
> *It doesn't matter what is read in the stars*
> *Or in the grounds of coffee*
> *My only wish*
> *Is your eyes*

A little party yesterday at home. The family, a few friends. The ambiance was rather gloomy.

What if the New Year is worse than the one that is ending? Poor Italy, Poor Europe.

But us . . . us, Clara, aren't we lucky?

Ti voglio bene.

*

In the new year, we finally met in Vienna. She was interviewing a composer whom I didn't know, but he seemed to be the darling of the moment, and had two tickets for the work he was directing, *Triptyque. Trois moments musicaux*. Pleasant but not unforgettable. Not really my taste, in any case. At dinner, she leant over the table and kissed my cheek. A loud kiss. Then I whispered my hotel-room number in her ear. She arrived with a playful smile. We were in each other's arms, caressing each other's face, and then our lips came together.

In my films, I've always avoided filming bodies frontally. The camera caressing the nakedness and then the 'performance' that happens with sighing and the obligatory sounds: there's nothing like it to destroy the myth of love-passion. The only time I could tolerate it was when Donald Sutherland and Julie Christie make love in Venice in *Don't Look Now*, the film by Nicolas Roeg. But that scene is real. Their desire had become so exacerbated during rehearsals that, during filming, they couldn't hold back. In the Seventies, that sort of thing was allowed. The cameras just kept rolling. As for the director, he couldn't believe his eyes. Devil's luck, that's what he had. That type of situation, needless to say, doesn't happen every day. And, when it doesn't happen, the symbolic approach is hardly convincing. The storm on the ocean, the musical crescendo, the wide angles on the waves, and then the sea that retreats and the calm on the beach again. Unless we are shown a close-up of a part of the agitating bodies, a sweaty back, a moving thigh. In general, film directors who are self-assured are very proud of those discoveries. One might object that it's the same thing in literature. That's why I'll be brief. The first time was so tender, so intense, that we were both astonished. Months later, she told me calmly: 'You know, I was resigned.

If it hadn't worked for us, well, too bad, we would have tried, that's all. And we would have been friends, without regrets.'

The following day, I was back in Rome, overcome with emotion. I can see myself back at my desk, trying to put some order into the plan for the screenplay, but incapable of doing anything. I was so overwhelmed that I even surprised myself by shedding a few tears—those tears of love that always seem so mysterious to me. I learnt later that she, too, was filled with whirling emotions. She had cried. In her car, going to have lunch in Bruges at her parents' house, the following Sunday, she had had to stop on a little dirt road. She turned off the car to cry in peace.

That was four years ago. Clara and I thought that our relationship would reach a plateauing curve. She hated that expression, but we needed to resolve ourselves to the idea. And yet . . . And yet, when got together, *la grotta*, the shadowy grotto between her legs, was always damp. We didn't get used to it. We still haven't. In any case, we stopped thinking about it. We became absorbed in deciphering the body of the other. With such passion that we could stay in bed for entire hours. Without getting bored. At least as far as I was concerned. Clara will have to write her own version.

Again, today, it happens that we adventure onto *terrae incognitae*. We make discoveries. Our minds are in unison. Often, we think the same things at the same moment. An additional proof that our intimacy is great, on every level. And we laugh. We laugh. Since we don't live together but in two distinct countries, the famous 'plateau' can't be seen. We don't feel guilty. Our love threatens no one. I think I've already said it, but it's important. We are both close to our spouse. We adore our children. We write to each other on *mature love*, our own social network. We talk on the phone almost every day. Does distance prevent fatigue? Clara thinks so. I'm not so sure, but I'm twenty years older than she. Whatever the case, our way of life is the only one imaginable. Practically, at least. We are happy, and, once again, I repeat, we are lucky.

*

My thoughts are wandering this pre-spring morning, a few weeks after our meeting in Vienna. I was in Umbria. I had been asked to be a member of the jury at a film festival—yet another. But what could be more enjoyable than to wander the austere alleys of a medieval town thinking of Clara? Escaping from the festival, I had found refuge in a cafe where I sipped a Brunello, my gaze lost in the rays of light on the wooden table, when I noticed a guy who was staring at me from another table. Exchange banalities on the festival with someone I didn't know—anything but that. I was going to stand up to pay and disappear, when the man spoke to me in an Italian that was painful to hear. He also laughed, a laugh that was vaguely familiar.

'*Ciao*! *Come sta?*'

He held out his hand.

'We've met, you know. You came to the house in Brussels. A dinner my wife, Clara, hosted . . . Anyway, if you don't remember, it doesn't matter. There was nothing memorable about that evening.'

It was her husband. The physicist. I then recognized him.

'Of course. How are you? Excuse me—I wasn't expecting to see you here. A meeting? A scientific colloquium?'

Again, he laughed that too-loud laugh. A smile would have sufficed.

'No, no, I'm here for the festival. Like you, but not on the jury. I'm presenting an American documentary denouncing drone warfare. Excellent, by the way.'

I couldn't stand listening to him speak Italian. To spare us both that, I mentally pushed the 'English' button.

'I didn't know you were involved politically.'

'Why not?'

I shrugged. He seemed upset. The tone of my voice, probably. I must have seemed pompous and overbearing.

'My dear friend, scientists are not always ignorant of the world in which we live. The world in which, if you'll allow me, each civilization incarnates a form of barbarism in the eyes of the others.'

I may have agreed with him, but his remark irritated me. I changed the subject.

'How is Clara?'

I don't know why I asked that question which sealed my fate. He insisted on going to another cafe to have something else. I would have liked to erase what I said but it was too late. I was under the spell of a morbid fascination. We were sitting across from each other. His cheeks were shining in the brightly lit cafe. He wanted to order wine. I didn't care which. He assured me that the Brunello was excellent, then resumed talking:

'How is Clara? That's your question. Well, I've never seen her so happy. And it's certainly not because of me. I analyse emotions as a scientist. Love is only a matter of molecules.'

He paused for a moment and laughed again, content with his witty phrase. I managed to smile weakly. I was hoping that my phone would ring. 'It's my wife,' I would excuse myself, I'm so sorry. And I would rush outside. But my phone didn't ring. I then imagined putting it on record. And later let Clara listen to this monologue. But that was probably not a good idea. In any case, I might be able to use a recording for a future short film—*Un pot à Spoleto*

I heard myself ask how they had met.

'It was twenty-four years ago. On a train. Her face looked intelligent. I was shocked that she was reading Simenon. I asked her why. Why him? "Because he's Belgian and I'm fed up with those pretentious French." I burst out laughing. She must have realized that her response was a bit stupid. She laughed, too, and I noticed that her breasts jumped like little animals in a cage. Simenon was a close friend of my father's. They played chess together every week. We exchanged phone numbers. Then I didn't leave her alone. Later, she admitted she married me because one of our friends had told her that I was Nobel Prize material. You laugh? Not me. Anyway, she wasn't joking, either.'

'What do you mean?'

He spread his arms in a gesture of resignation.

'I think she fell out of love the day she understood it was too late for Stockholm.'

'That's hard to believe.'

'Let's just say that, after the twins were born, a certain lassitude set in. Don't misunderstand me. We're very close. It even happens that we still experience bouts of passion. Like lightning in a sky whose colour would be, how to put it, a bit too uniform . . . However, for several years we've been concentrating on our work. She adores the radio, you know. I'm sure that her voice alone causes masses of listeners to swoon. So things are good. We're fine. But I still have to wonder what is making her so happy. Even the children say that they've never seen her so relaxed. I tell myself that the passing of time . . . At our ages, we're finally out of adolescence, right? What about you, Giangiacomo? Are you happy?'

The time had come to put an end to this exchange. I looked at my watch and pretended I had an appointment. He smiled with a knowing look. I didn't feel guilty in the least. Ron was in his bubble. Warm. I called Clara while I was going back to the hotel. At first, she couldn't get over the fact that we had had coffee together. I told her the details of our conversation and she laughed. I was happy to imagine her laughing.

I had also recorded our first interview on my phone. I like to keep a record of what I say to the media. Sometimes I play it over for myself. Like she does, moreover. We have fun with this formal side. That evening, at the hotel, I listened to it for the nth time.

C. *There are moments when your last feature film resembles a film from the Sixties. The black and white, the way of filming, hand-held camera, long shots fixed on landscapes . . . Is this an homage to a specific filmmaker?*

Me. *No, not really, I often re-watch Fellini's 8 ½ and Tarkovski's* Stalker. *I really like New Wave film. Both French and Czech. And since his films are housed there, somewhere in my brain, it is completely plausible that you'll see echoes of them.*

C. *And Gramsci's love life? It is essentially absent from your film. In general, moreover, there's not a lot of love in your works. Why?*

Me. *Because love is a pastime for adolescents. A form of narcissism, as Freud would say. A sign of immaturity. To bring it to the screen, you'd have to be able to express the vulnerability, the weakness, the inner chaos. Moreover, Gramsci's sexuality is of no particular interest. But you're right. Generally, I avoid exhibitionism. And the boredom that goes with it. Today, nothing is left to the imagination. As for me, I prefer the low-cut blouse of Silvana Mangano in* Bitter Rice. *To glimpse the glorious outline of a breast inspires me more than a completely naked body. Other than that, what did you think of the cinematography? Isn't it more interesting than sex?*

C. *I liked your framing, your magnificent and oppressive Sardinian skies.*

Me. *A bit like you?*

C. *Like me?*

Me. *Sorry. I take that back. It's your eyes that made me say that. Passion and fragility. Your eyes are vulnerable.*

C. *OK, hmmm . . . I think I have everything I need. The interview is over.*

Sometimes, tired of working, we would stretch out on a sofa and yawn contentedly in each other's arms. She would pinch my hip. Did I still think love was just an adolescent disturbance?

'Not ours. Ours is as ripe as a fleshy fruit. Of a different kind.'

'And yet, dear friend, you are quick to behave like an adolescent. You pout, you show signs of jealousy . . .'

She was still staring at me with that same playful air.

'For example?'

'Yesterday, when Ron called, that annoyed you . . . '

'Of course, we were . . . we were just getting started . . . it was the fact of being interrupted, nothing to do with him.'

'Of course, of course,' she said, sounding like someone who didn't believe it.

Today, I turned seventy. Everyone made an effort to celebrate the event. At Titti's there were fifty people, family and friends. Titti and my wife had talked about the menu for three days. I have the impression it wasn't easy. My son took care of the wine. Since that's the crucial element, I insisted on tasting it. Titti grudgingly opened a bottle. I looked at the label. A sepia photo with the legend *Gramsci 1920*. I laughed. OK, it was good. But, a pity, one person was missing. The most noticeable of all when she's not around.

I've always celebrated birthdays every ten years. *Non è il mio forte*. This one in particular. I'm in good shape on a personal level. Clara has transformed my life by breathing an unimaginable happiness into it. It is intellectually that things aren't great. I feel drained. Europe is ill. Italy in particular. Blocked arteries like those of its eighty-something president, Giorgio Napolitano. Out of breath, looking desperately for a surgeon to do a triple bypass on him. Or to implant a German heart in him.

Clara cheered me up. She suggested we leave for a few days to celebrate this birthday in our own way. As always, she found a dream location. I went to Fiumicino to pick her up and then we drove forty kilometres or so outside of Rome. It was cold, but there was a fire in that *agriturismo* villa where we stayed. With the peaceful music of waves outside. We had a light dinner. Almost a picnic. The Gramsci cru made her laugh, she wanted to know the true name. Her husband's fiftieth birthday was coming up soon. 'You could call it *Belated*

Nobel 1962.' Again, she laughed. Her true laugh. The one that always makes me want to kiss her.

The next day, we took a walk on the deserted beach, not talking. Before I could ask her what she was thinking, she tightened her grip on my arm. And said in a very soft voice:

'You know, I'm a bit afraid. This need for you, it keeps getting stronger. You had told me that it would taper off. That it would reach a plateau. Your famous plateau on which we could swing peacefully, like in a hammock. While going from one emotion to another, like in Beethoven's sonatas. Well? Where is your damned plateau?'

It was difficult to respond, I felt exactly the same. I simply reiterated a golden rule of *mature love*. Don't do any harm to anyone. The opposite of a novel by García Márquez. Clara pointed out that, for us, love and life were twisted together like branches of a vine. That is why, even when we couldn't see each other, it was so necessary that we talk on the phone. To really talk. Sometimes one or two hours on the phone. She reminded me that *mature love* was really nice, but that sometimes she really felt like being immature. To run off with me. To elope without a trace. I admitted that I, too, really wanted that.

'Keep in mind, if we did that, it would perhaps be the end of our problem. You know what Ambrose Bierce said, "*Love is a temporary insanity curable by marriage*"?'

'I know that's your theory. But I've already told you: in our case, I'm not so sure.'

Silence. We kissed. A long, winter kiss. A kiss that sustains the body. Then we headed to the villa in quest of the lunch that would do the same.

'No,' I told her. 'You know well that, if we lived together, there's another problem that would arise.'

She stopped.

'Which one?'

'The one that is raised when love is no longer but a long plaint.'

'*Che vuoi dire?*'

'That for *amore maturo* the only plateau is the grave.'

'Oh, stop Gigi. I hate talking like that.'

'*Amore*, the laws of biology are incontrovertible.'

'Be quiet!'

At the end of this exchange, as with so many others, I held her closely against me. I held her tightly for so long that our senses were awakened. Back at the hotel, we made love before lunch. Then, since it was winter, our nap lasted awhile. And, in the evening, we found ourselves in a little neighbouring village, sitting at a table in front of a steaming minestrone, grilled fish and a bottle of Brunello.

'No desert,' she said in a formal tone. 'Some mint tea will be perfect.' But when we returned to our room and I kissed her, I knew that she had snuck the little chocolate that came with her tea.

In those places—it was true for all the places where we were together—we created our own little personal cosmos.

Not that the exterior world seemed threatening to us. But, suddenly, it just seemed dull. Boring. The tenderness that connected us was such that, when we were together, we became impermeable to the rest. And that tenderness resisted time. It resisted everything. It didn't leave. And we knew it. We knew it so well that we were at peace. Nothing threatened us. *Amore maturo* resists all fears that immature love usually carries with it.

And what anguish, when you think of it. What torture. The passion of young Werther leads him to suicide. He thinks that the great inner fire will reduce everything to ashes in any case, and that it's better to immediately be done with it. Charlotte has to leave to escape the flames. And I won't mention what impossible love did to Juliette and her Romeo— we're in very Romantic waters there, it's true. But non-romantic love, what is it? To a revolutionary apprentice who had sought refuge with her in Paris, Marguerite Duras said one day that love and revolution were 'two views of the mind'. She informed her, just like that, as an aside. That happened during the events of May 1968. Love seemed synonymous with youth at the time. For Clara and me, that's no longer the case.

One day, Clara borrowed *Un homme et une femme*, the Lelouch film, from the library at the radio station. I hadn't seen it for decades. We both had the music in our heads, obviously, the famous *Chabadabada*. And the car races. But that was just about it. We watched it in bed, on her computer, in one of our favourite hideouts—was it in Paris? The film is still fascinating. Anouk Aimée and Trintignant are both in the flower of their youth. And both are stricken with sadness. He has lost his wife, and she her husband. And since they both have a child in the same boarding school in Deauville, they fall in love, necessarily. But it is complicated, necessarily. The first time they're in bed together, she is unable to get out of her mind images of her husband who died in a car accident on a winding road. No orgasm.

'It's likely that the problem wouldn't have arisen if Lelouch had kept the husband and wife alive,' I noted to Clara.

'You mean, like for us? Like in real life? But Lelouch, at that time, could he have made a film with us?'

'Why not? I've always thought that *Anna Karenina* would have been less stereotypical if the woman had married Vronski and if she had fallen madly in love with Karinin. And if gay marriage had been allowed, wouldn't Shakespeare have had an interest in reworking *Othello* so Desdemona kills Iago? And Proust's Albertine? With really muscular shoulders . . . I bet you anything that Proust would have turned her into a man.'

As always, I said all that to make her laugh. And it worked. Then I kissed her lips.

At six in the morning, her phone rang. She seemed surprised and annoyed. I guessed what had happened. I got up, shaved. I took a shower and put on my clothes. She was sitting on the edge of the bed, her head in her hands. A literary scandal had just broken in Belgium. Suddenly, I wanted to know more about it. A scandal? In Belgium? A woman she knew had written her autobiography. In it she told how during the war the Belgian police had arrested her parents and sent them to Auschwitz. How the little six-year-old girl she was at the time had got it into her head to set off on foot to look for them. How she had headed in the direction of Germany, and how, when she got lost in a forest, she had been rescued, adopted and saved by wolves. The book had been an immediate best-seller. But her publisher had just announced that he had been duped. Everything about the story was false. The woman wasn't Jewish, her parents had given up the ghost peacefully in their bed. And no wolf had ever taken pity on that ridiculous Little Red Riding Hood. In short, the publisher demanded that she give back the astronomical royalties he had paid—which, I pointed out to Clara, were pretty miserly, all the same.

'Listen, my Clara, all that she did was to enter the game of the market, and she played it. I should buy the rights to that book and make a movie out of it . . .'

'Too late. And don't you find that disgusting?'

'No. Opportunistic, amoral, amusing, done to attract attention and money, of course. But not disgusting. The Holocaust has become an industry, that woman wanted to profit from it, that's all.'

'I absolutely don't agree with you. But I still have to interview her at 2 p.m.'

'Invite her over. Tell her to join us and we can question her together. But, please, no moral judgement. She is not the first, and won't be the last. The Holocaust business is an

American and European phenomenon. She did it to make some money, not to hurt anyone. Don't you want to come back to bed?'

That was out of the question. We had breakfast, then she took a plane for Brussels. And me? I found a cafe and began to make notes. I don't know why, but the 'atrocious' Belgian story took me back to the death of my father. To the circumstances of his death. How? Why? Had he really been killed by fascist bullets? The more I thought about it, the more I doubted. The war was over. Most of the *camicie nere* were making peace with Christian Democracy. How would it be in their interest to cause an incident that would draw attention to them? Was it possible that no one knew the identity of the assassin or assassins?

My mother. Of course my mother knew. She knew everything. Why didn't she say anything? Something didn't add up in her version. Was it she? Could she have killed him? No. Impossible. She was his closest collaborator. And yet, the mystery persisted. In those days, anything was possible. I thought about the photo of them that I always kept above my desk. The Resistance years. They both seemed happy. In my father's face there was something mischievous. As for my mother, she was laughing a laugh that I couldn't define.

Recently, I watched *Rashomon*, the masterpiece by Kurosawa, again. Maybe that was the right way to approach the enigma. Tell about the murder in four different ways and let the viewer come up with his own idea. Yes. That's how I was going to tackle it. My film would be a double homage. First, to my parents, and also to the Japanese master, who, like them, was a communist. I called Clara to tell her about my idea. She was someplace where we kept getting cut off. I sent her a text and she immediately responded in French: *Bonne idée*. I wondered what she really thought. Maybe she thought that this was just another of my fantasies. One of those thousands of ideas that bubble incessantly in my brain, simmering without producing anything before ending definitively down the drain. I went back to making notes. So as to prove to her that, this time, that wouldn't be the case.

As I was covering the pages with black ink, I began to realize the stumbling block I would have to overcome. I would have to paint the Italy of that time, the one that my parents had described to me. To show that, in the Mussolini years, Italy was a complex country, torn apart, where, as I often repeated to Clara, the Resistance was only another name for civil war. A war that continued even after the German attempt to save the regime.

I called Pietro, an old historian friend. He was unequivocal. 'Don't write anything before reading Pavone. You won't find a more detailed portrait of the civil war anywhere . . . Better yet, go see him. He's still alive, you know.'

Go to find out why. Even before I was able to think about Pietro's advice, a wave of *yearning* came over me. Without warning. The kind that swells and grows to such a degree that it can wipe out an entire day. Then it is impossible to do anything. The feeling of missing overwhelmed me. Sometimes, it even happened, bizarrely, when we were together. Excessive melancholia. That one was huge. A Hokusai wave, a tsunami. VVVHYL. But Clara was with her family, and no telephone, no calming balm, no sedative was foreseeable.

Until then I hadn't talked about Clara to anyone except Bi. But I figured that with Pietro I could unburden myself, and I took him to Titti's.

My generation has a lot of defects, but it isn't *judgmental*, as they say. Everything but moralistic or preaching.

'And how did that begin?' Pietro asked.

I told him every detail.

'My friend, it's a lovely story, but completely nuts.'

'*Mature love.*'

'If you'll allow me, you don't exactly strike me as someone very mature. Rather, you sound like an old teenager in a depression.'

'Some symptoms are the same, regardless of age.'

'You should make a film out of it. It would be more original than Gramsci or the civil war. And if you really want to do your Resistance story, you can always incorporate flashbacks.'

I wouldn't budge.

'Never in your life. If I do a film on the idea of *mature love*, there won't be any turning back. It's incomparable, you understand. A question of intensity . . .'

Pietro and I have been friends for fifty years. At a certain point we lost track of each other. Carried away by the wave of the Sixties, he'd landed on the shores of the far-left, in the wake of Toni Negri. At the time, I was, myself, immersed in the universe of filmmaking. And then Pietro had reappeared, regretting the absurdity of his political adventures. A bit of luck: he hadn't been blacklisted anywhere. He was given a position teaching philosophy in a high school in Rome, and has been doing great ever since. Intellectually, but not only. And we confided in each other, the way we used to do in the preceding century.

'In your opinion, how is it going to end?'

'*Morto stecchito. Come un cadavere.*'

'Do you think so? What does she say?'

'She hates thinking about it. Anyway, I've always told her that if, for one reason or another, it all becomes too burdensome, she just has to tell me. I would disappear on tiptoe.'

'Really?'

'I repeat—In *amore maturo*, there is a *maturo*, that means mature.'

'Mature, death . . . Death would be better, no?'

'On the condition that nothing is dragged out. A quick heart attack. A bolt of lightning.'

We both laughed. We ordered another drink. Then we said goodbye to Titti.

Clara

And now? I felt like an idiot. What was I going to do with all that? I was sitting there, in front of the neon-green thumb drive that Elvira had given me, and the pile of scattered papers I had just read. I kept looking first at one, then the other. I couldn't think of anything. Empty. An empty vessel, that's what I was. Even throwing myself into the sea seemed futile. No more messages to send. Gigi was dead. *Punto finale. Punto morto.*

It was as if a little glacial wind had begun to blow. Sweeping away everything in its path. So, writing in the middle of the wind . . . Elvira had talked about an agreement. But it wasn't like that, the agreement between Gigi and me. Gigi didn't have to go like that. Without warning. Three little spins and then *ciao*. A few *Goldberg Variations* and *ci vediamo*. But where, when, in which other life? Ordinarily, we would have discussed this book together. It was a two-person game. A fantasy with four hands. I would sometimes see it as a secret place. Like a trunk in which we would have eagerly hidden, taking them out another day, all the souvenirs from trips, remembrances of frolicking and debates, bits of conversations, arguments, reproaches, wild laughter . . . all the little bits of coloured and necessarily a bit-fetishized thread with which our story was woven. Each person would have chosen and brought their own, like offerings that believers come to place in Buddhist temples. One day, we would have opened the trunk together. It would have been a motley collection. It would have awakened a hotchpotch of emotions, buried, discordant. We wouldn't have agreed. We would have relived it all. That's what writing is for.

'What you say about Stockholm, it's a bit much, *my darling*.'

'Why? What did I write? That you were sulking?'

'*Are you kidding*? You *were sulking* . . .'

'You insisted that I do a piece to the glory of Irma in a programme on Florence and intellectuals. Her great book on Boccaccio. For the septuacentennial anniversary of his birth . . . And *The Decameron*, you kept saying. That pure masterpiece that has been completely forgotten! And so cheerful, as you say. Your Belgian listeners must certainly know the *Decameron*!'

I protested. That wasn't my angle.

'Gigi . . .'

But you weren't listening to me. You interrupted me. You continued, full steam ahead.

'Why don't you tell them the very funny scene of Masetto with the nuns? The handsome, young Masetto who, in order to be hired as a gardener in a convent—as a gardener, but not just that—pretends he can neither hear nor speak . . . '

That was it, you were off, and you were already laughing, yourself. You continued.

'Masetto knows well that, even though you're a nun, that doesn't mean you're made of stone. He ends up in the garden shed with the nuns in his arms. They all troop in and out of the shed. Including the Mother Superior. Boccaccio even writes that the abbess is all too happy to experience that sweetness which she criticized in others until then . . . Or something like that. He has a phrase . . . Anyway, it reaches a point so that during one encounter Masetto is no longer able to perform. He begs for mercy, so to speak.'

You never tired of that passage where Masetto explains to the abbess that a cock is enough for ten hens, but that he, at that pace, would never 'endure'. And you rolled your eyes imitating the terrified nun: 'What is this? I thought you were mute!'

But I was in no mood to laugh. I knew that *The Decameron* was one of your favourite books. That scene, in particular. You had told me that you read it constantly in Sardinia when you were a teenager. In hiding. And that it inspired you a lot. That *le pagine di Masetto* were even stuck together in your original copy.

But that evening, Boccaccio and his fake-mute no longer amused me. Hearing all that even put me in a worse mood. I had the impression you were using me. And what's more, to promote your wife! Her brilliant book! That was really too much.

'So that was really it, a little spurt of jealousy? I spent the whole evening asking you what was wrong. *Che succeso?* You spent the whole evening sullen and silent. You were frowning. And, under those eyebrows your green eyes shot out bolts of black.'

What you don't know is that when we finally went to bed—in that charming attic room that looked out over a little square, Gamla Stan, remember?—I wanted to tell you what was wrong. Because, deep down, I was mad at myself for being jealous. To ruin the little bit of time we had together. I made a huge effort. I thought I was being heroic. I gathered together my ideas and my courage—it's hard to admit when you're jealous. Jealous of the wife of your lover! I prepared what I was going to say. You turned your back to me in bed, I couldn't see you—anyway, we might have already turned out the light. I was thinking of what Freud said: *it is brighter in the dark when someone speaks.* Something like that.

'OK, Gigi, listen . . . '

At that moment I heard snoring. You had already fallen asleep. I was angry. More than angry. Then I, too, turned over facing the other side of the bed, hating you even more.

I don't know why that scene is coming back to me now. A tiff between clandestine lovers. A scene of non-marriage. Memories come back to us following a strange logic. And now mysterious currents have tossed me from the North Sea to the Gulf of the Angels. I now see us in Sardinia, in your village. Sitting on the little white bench in front of Marcello's bar.

Looking out at the sea, at the lagoon, at the infinite shades of blue.

'Gigi! *Clara bella*! *Cosa vi porto?*'

I'm sitting, my legs crossed, my back against the wall, in my damp swimsuit under my African pareo. You're looking at my legs and my knees browned by the sun, a pouting face as you often have by letting a little air pass out from your upper lip. Then telling me once again that I should start paying attention because, in fact, I was becoming too thin, and that . . .

'*Che cosa le servo?*'

'*Rosso . . . Cannonau. Grazie, Marcello.*'

It was there, at Marcello's, that we had talked about this book project for the first time. Whose idea was it? Yours? Mine? Perhaps mine, with my obsession with holding on to anything that might have mattered. You kept nothing. You really didn't care, and then you would lose everything. Not only your watch, your glasses and your mobile phone which you always left in every taxi. You admitted once that you had lost a film of an interview with Rossellini. A long dialogue that you had had with him, and that you had filmed.

'You really can't find it?' I had asked, frustrated.

'No . . . I know, it upsets me, too. But . . . the recording wasn't good. Mainly the sound. Bad quality.'

You had shrugged with an air of fatality. Then you changed the subject.

But let's go back to this four-handed book project. So, we were there, at Marcello's. A bit earlier, in the afternoon, we would have made love. Then a siesta. You had told me that there were all sorts of siestas for Romans.

'At least three or four.'

'Really?'

'Oh, yes . . . You're thinking about the very simple *siesta*. But that, in the collective imaginary, is the Mexican siesta, if you see what I mean. The standard Italian siesta is *il pisolino*. Not to be confused with *il pisellino*, which means a little pee-pee or peas.'

'That's it, of course . . .'

'I'm serious, Clara. *Il pisello* is a normal pee-pee. Similarly, if you ask me for *una coccola*—a cuddle—be careful not to use the wrong vowel, because *una caccola* is a dried piece of snot.'

'Gigi, please, how old are you?'

'You need to know these things, *amore*. It's basic vocabulary. Then there's the Roman siesta, *la pennichella*. And we've even invented *l'abbiocco*, which is . . . the desire for a siesta!'

'I love this country. The pinnacle of civilization!'

So we were at Marcello's, after *la pennichella* or whatever it was (there must have been a Sardinian term, too, but I've forgotten it), we must have talked and talked. As usual. Then I would have ended up telling you:

'You know, I've finished . . .'

'Finished? *Non è possibile*! I really thought that I would never read that part . . . '

In the way your sentence lingered on. I would have heard everything you were thinking. That I was slow, really too slow. That I should have made an effort to write a long time ago. That I didn't need to be afraid. Nor to consult a ton of useless papers. That we were doing this for fun. That's also what I loved about you. *Il piacere prima di tutto.* What counted most was pleasure. Our good pleasure. The one we would take in writing together. Joy, enjoyment. A quasi-religion of delight.

'Well, show me, quickly . . .' you would have said to me.

Back at home, I would have sent you the text. To gigi.maturelove@alice.it, that secret address you had really insisted on creating for us. Even when we were together, we would send email messages, from either side of the bed, with our laptops open on our knees.

You would have begun to read while I went down to the beach—because it was better than anxiously looking for your reaction. And because yes, in spite of everything, at my age, I still gave you what I was doing, my show plans, interviews, documentaries, videos . . . as if you were meant to evaluate and grade them.

In the evening, we would have discussed all that.

'Really? . . . No, tell me the truth, Gigi, the real truth. Did you like the text?'

'You know that I can't lie to you.'

I would have been relieved. You would have continued:

'So you were really thinking about Irma when we had the Stockholm fight? Wow, I hadn't understood it like that at all . . .'

Or you would have grumbled:

'There are, all the same, some places where you exaggerate. Claiming I snore. Anyway, I really wonder why you still have such a bad memory of that city.'

'You had taught me your Sardinian grandmother's recipe for bean soup, remember?'

'Exactly, so why reduce everything to that incident?'

You would have said that that deserved punishment, that your vengeance would be pitiless.

I would have challenged you, singing:

'*Parole, parole, parole . . .* '

'You'll see . . . '

I would have said:

'OK. Wonderful, I'm waiting.'

Then I would have pinched the skin on your hips making you cry out. I would have scrunched my nose while staring deep into your eyes. And, as punishment, I would have ended up drinking your glass of Cannonau.

Morto. Good God, Gigi, what were you thinking? *Perdio, come ti è venuta l'idea?*

No, I wasn't in the mood, obviously, to write anything. Even for Elvira, even for your beloved daughter. I picked up the sheets of paper and put the neon-green thumb drive on top; that drive was somewhat transparent, as if one could see directly into its insides . . . Then I got up to fix some coffee, trying not to think that that coffee—'a very special variety of

Ethiopian beans'—it was you, again, who had given it to me. We had bought it together in Brussels, in that tiny little shop, that miniscule cafe on Spoormarketsstraat, one of the rare places in Belgium where the coffee was up to snuff in your Italian opinion. I stood up trying not to think that, from now on, my miniscule Roman flat was going to become something like an encyclopedia of you. An encyclopedia of you without you.

In no mood to write. *Basta così.*

Ten days must have gone by. At the RTBF, I had said that I was taking a vacation and, at home, that I was staying in Rome for work. A report on a film shoot. The new feature film by Paolo Sorrentino. Ron, in any case, was at a colloquium organized by CERN in Geneva. A very high-level international symposium whose title I quickly forgot. He was the *keynote speaker* and had been preparing for it for a long time. I was grateful to Elvira for not calling me again. I needed to be alone. And to understand exactly how alone I was, I needed an even greater solitude.

Anyway, even if I had wanted to talk, to whom would I have talked? Gigi and I had been incredibly careful during those four years. No one knew. At least as far as I know. Sometimes, when Gigi joined me in Brussels or elsewhere, I asked:

'So where are you?'

'Well, in Brussels, as you see.'

'Come on . . . officially, Gigi . . . what are you doing?'

'A lecture on the use of video by autochthonous populations in South America. It's titled, *Between Appropriation and Acculturation: The Influence of Globalization on Amerindian Cinema.*'

I burst out laughing. He always had a knack for inventing the craziest titles. Gigi was a born storyteller. And, of course, a seducer. He couldn't be telling me that Irma . . .

He sighed.

'No, *carissima*. Irma and I, it's not like you and Ron. Not at all. I've explained that already a hundred times. Because of my . . . let's say, my earlier escapades, it's been a long time since Irma . . . Oh, my darling, you can see what I mean. Don't force me . . .'

I protested.

'That's not true, Gigi. A woman never completely doesn't care about her husband's affairs.'

'You're not an affair. In any case, calm down, all is well at home . . .'

And Gigi pulled me to him, holding me in his arms. As if he were declaring an end to the conversation.

A conversation that was now, indeed, over for good. There was no one with whom to continue it. No one with whom to remember it. The secret that enveloped me like a thick winter coat weighing me down. Before, it was rather light. We could even laugh about it. Play with it. But now . . . I was thinking: maybe this is the price I must pay. The price our society, without our even knowing it, makes clandestine lovers pay for their illicit loves. Society's way of saying: 'Until the end of your days, you will be alone with your secret. You will never say anything about it. Not a thing, under threat of shame or damnation. You will hide it in perpetuity. You will take it to your grave.' Yes, that was it, *the* punishment. King Midas . . . It's strange that no one, in real life, ever mentions him.

Possibly, Elvira. Elvira might have been the only one with whom I could have . . . Elvira and . . . you, Gigi. At that moment, I left the kitchen and opened the door to my office. I took the computer, the very thin Mac that you gave me at the beginning of our 'marriage'. I sat down on the little terrace that looks out over the Piazza del Popolo. And I wrote to your secret address.

From: Clara, clara.maturelove@alice.it
To: Gigi, gigi.maturelove@alice.it
Date: *13 settembre 2014*

In the subject line I put one line. Four letters.
YLVH

I wrote: *Yearning Level Very High. But you don't care. You really don't care.* Then I closed the computer.

At that moment, under my windows, some young people were singing. On the terrace of Canova, three men were arguing while the sun was disappearing behind the obelisk. Santa Maria dei Miracoli, do something for me, I thought. All of a sudden, my throat tightened. I passed my index finger mechanically over the cover of the computer, over the edge of the soft, white apple. And I cried.

I don't know how to explain that, suddenly, in the following days, I started writing to you again. I couldn't stop myself. I had decided to do what you did, you remember, the year I had gone skiing with my sons and husband in Colorado. You kept 'A Diary of Absence' (that's what you called it, I think). You weren't expecting any responses, but you sent me messages, thoughts, your readings of the *Corriere*—which invariably made you mad—your usual bad jokes, the ones that masked your worries: everything that could kill time and your impatience. You hated it when we couldn't talk. Thanks to that journal, you were with me even without me. It is only natural that I do the same. *Il diario di una mancanza.* Is that how you'd say it? The diary of an absence. *Un assenza infinita.*

From: Clara, clara.maturelove@alice.it
To: Gigi, gigi.maturelove@alice.it
Subject: *Diario di una mancanza*
Date: 17 settembre 2014

If you're the one who sent that to me, it's really not cool. Look at what I found in my mail this morning. A brochure for *Comparto funerario Comune città di Roma.* An ad for *funerals at discount prices.* With a choice of *funerary processions, exhumations, cremations, transportation of the deceased with or without a coffin* (obviously at different prices), *anywhere in Italy/abroad,* and a *funerary advisor (State certified)* also able to take care of *conservation, preparation, dressing, refrigeration table, etc.* Do you understand what a refrigeration table is doing in all of that?

I know it's morbid, but listen to this: *Funerary room with welcome area, salons and departure room.* That's what confused me the most, the *departure room.* I suddenly saw again all the salons, the lounges where we waited for so many departures. You and I. So many take-offs to elsewheres where you'd be. Or not . . . Like the day when you almost missed the plane for Skyros in Athens. I tried to make the Aegean Airlines hostess understand that you were coming, right away, that I had just spoken to you on the phone, that the flight from Rome was delayed, but that you were there, at Eleftherios-Venizelos, and that you were running to us, to Gate 32 where she was tapping her foot impatiently because, she had already told me, it's time, Madame . . . Time to finish boarding . . . I kept saying that I had just seen you at the end of the corridor, you were coming, you were running, you were out of breath and, no, no, the bus that would take us to the plane couldn't leave without you, it wasn't possible. I had put my foot in the door to prevent it from shutting, and I begged the driver—a real Greek tragedian. Then the stewardess said:

'If you see your husband arriving, describe him to me. What is he wearing?'

I really liked that she called you my husband. The way I liked it when I arrived at hotels and at the reception desk you had told them that 'your wife was coming'. I said you were tall with salt-and-pepper hair, but since I didn't know what you were wearing that day, she probably thought I was bluffing, and wasn't convinced.

'*I'm sorry, Madame. It's impossible to wait any longer,*' she said with her strong Greek accent.

She closed the gate. The bus left, and I found myself alone in the plane next to your empty seat.

On Olympus, the gods must have been sympathetic. It began to rain so hard that the plane was stuck on the tarmac. Right before the end of the storm, you burst in, your tall profile bent down in the door frame in the front of the plane. Your raincoat was dripping. A scene from a movie so clichéd that you would never have filmed it. A bit out of breath, but no more than that, you smiled at me. A wide smile. And you said to me:

'*Ciao amore. Grazie alla pioggia!*'

You didn't seem stressed. Later, you admitted that at Fiumicino, seeing that the Athens flight was delayed and that the little two-engine plane to Skyros made the trip only twice a week, you were really scared. Our days were numbered. The weather had saved us.

Why am I thinking about all that again? Oh, yes. *Departure room*. I looked at the many models of tombstones—for example, the #11, the Ruby Star model. Dim: 130 x 230 cm in Jelena granite. Price: 3,170 euros, including placement (instead of 3,600, that price is struck out, a bargain). What's funniest is . . . guess what the company who makes them is called? . . . Marbrerie Lhorphelin! I don't know what Irma has chosen for you, *my love*. I will never know. I won't go to visit you at the cemetery, I don't do that. And when I say that I don't know what Irma has chosen, I savour, as you know I would, the fact of not having to take care of anything. *Donna invisibile*. For once, this status as an invisible woman has an advantage . . .

From: Clara, clara.maturelove@alice.it
To: Gigi, gigi.maturelove@alice.it
Subject: *Diario di una mancanza*
Date: *18 settembre 2014*

I know why you had that brochure sent to me, Gigi. Because of that part of me that has always been interested in the invisible links between the dead and the living. The way in which they communicate. I remember a conversation when you made great fun of me on this subject. You, the fake rational. I was coming back from I'm not sure which work trip. Laos, Vietnam, maybe Korea. I had seen shamans, I couldn't contain myself. I compared their beliefs to those of magical realism in South America, the Ashkenazi tradition of Eastern Europe, African animism . . .

'Do you realize? There are, all the same, quite a few people on this planet who believe that the dead are there, that they inhabit objects or that they circulate amongst us.'

Now, it's you who are wandering around my postbox and my inbox. And, even if you don't react, I'm sure that you're not unhappy to receive my news. OK, right, it's not very funny, but I'm hanging on to anything that can help me, you see. It's the best I could find to keep going.

From: Clara, clara.maturelove@alice.it
To: Gigi, gigi.maturelove@alice.it
Subject: *Diario di una mancanza*
Date: *20 settembre 2014*

I need to answer Elvira. I'm going to do it. Find the strength. Tell her that, no, I won't write my 'part'. That she was right, I won't be honouring the 'contract'. Not now, in any case. I'm sure she'll understand. However, in thinking about it, there are many things I'd like her to know. *Delle cose importanti.* About women, faithfulness, conjugal love, conjugated loves. You see, Gigi, if I had one, I would tell my daughter those things—I would at least try to get her to feel those things. Since I don't have one, I have to find a way to suggest them to yours. Not my 'part', but . . . Notes, maybe. It's dangerous, I know. At twenty-five, one is still young. However, if she reads them one day, maybe they'll open doors for her. Doors to other ways of loving and being loved.

From: Clara, clara.maturelove@alice.it
To: Gigi, gigi.maturelove@alice.it
Subject: *Diario di una mancanza*
Date: *1 ottobre 2014*

Voilà. I've actually put my ideas down on paper. For your Elvira. Do you think she'll be shocked if she reads it all?

> Gigi was a great hedonist. Maybe I shouldn't tell you that, Elvira, but it's no secret to anyone. Everyone in the film world knew his reputation as a *womanizer*. Wait. I'm trying to think of an equivalent in Italian, but I'm not able to come up with anything. It doesn't matter. Forgive me, I'm going to talk to you the way Gigi and I did. Mixing languages, English, Italian—and mainly French, since, you at least, speak it. Poor Gigi. He would sometimes try, when we were in Brussels together. To make me happy. But what torture for my ears! He asked if he should study it. I never managed

to encourage him. As for you, please forgive my mistakes in Italian. I can't prevent myself from using it here and there. I scatter it everywhere in these notes. It's my way of still being with him.

But let's get back to him. To the man who loved women. Because that's what really comes back to me first. Not the list of conquests. The catalogue, *Mille tre* . . . Not the cynical Don Juan. No. A man who sincerely loved 'his' women, listened to them, cherished them, was interested in them. Don't judge him too harshly, I'm sure all were very happy when they were with him. All except perhaps Irma. I know, he told me. And you must know, too. When, before they got married, he was courting your mother madly, she had asked him three questions:

'Do you really love me?'

'Will you cheat on me?'

'Will you make me suffer?'

Gigi had answered yes to the first two questions. He was sincere, I'm sure of it and, since it was the Seventies, Irma had appreciated his transparency concerning the inevitable affairs to come. The situation became more difficult when, a few years later, at a film shoot, Gigi met Nadia. Nadia the dark-haired, Italian actress of immense sensuality. I think it was during the filming of *I Vicoli*. You know that film your father made? Yes, of course. I love it. In short, for the first time since Irma, Gigi was in love, even madly in love.

And so he constructed a parallel life, but one day it ended up weighing on him. Because he had a gripping desire to run off with that girl, but, at the same time, he wasn't absolutely sure that he wanted to.

After a few years of keeping their affair a secret, Nadia, who was unmarried, began to put unbearable pressure on him. The classic scenario. And Gigi, who could be a coward, couldn't decide what to do. All he could decide was to talk about it to Irma. An earthquake in their marriage. The entire family was shaken. Because they had decided—and I think they did the right thing—to tell you children about it. That crisis is the one Gigi alludes to in his part of the story. You couldn't not have recognized it. He told me that, in the end, he promised never to 'see' Nadia, as we say. And that, in your home, there was overall relief. But, one day, that woman asked him to take her somewhere by car. He told me that he had agreed because he couldn't do otherwise—was he lying? Was he still secretly seeing her? I never tried to find out. In any case, on the way, he ran into you. You were walking out of your art school. You had your backpack hanging off one shoulder, it was swinging nonchalantly, when you noticed him at the wheel of his black Alfa Romeo.

'Elvira seemed so happy to see me,' Gigi told me when he was telling me about that scene. 'You wouldn't believe it, I can still see her smile. Beaming. But suddenly she saw Nadia sitting in the passenger seat, and she immediately understood. Her face became pale. She gave me a look . . . A look I will never forget.'

Believe me, Elvira, when he told me that years later, Gigi still had goosebumps. He was angry at himself and he knew he would be angry at himself forever for having inflicted that on you. I don't know how he originally responded to Irma's third question. But the response from the facts no longer held any doubt— even less so because Nadia and Irma, to round out a bad film, knew each other rather well and even liked each other. Often the case.

But I do believe that that incident was isolated. From that time, he really took great care to never again make his women—wife, daughter, friends, mistresses—suffer . . . It had become an obsession . . . I know it must have been a shock for you to come across the notebook. It had to be. You put yourself in Irma's place and all that past must have made you sick. But, I repeat, don't judge him too quickly. Nor too harshly.

I'm telling you all this while thinking about my sons. Twins. They are younger than you, but I'm always struck when I hear them talking with clear disgust: 'X cheated on Y.' Whereas, in their tales, X and Y are going out together, as they say, but nothing more. But, it's always categorical. 'Y was right to *break it off*, you understand . . . you really can't do that . . .' It seems that your generation is particularly 'judgmental'. Are you, too? Do you judge Gigi and me harshly?

How did you feel when you read these pages? I know how much Gigi loved you, Elvira, but, in the end, I don't know anything about you. And yet, I have a tendency to tell myself that there is something else. You must have felt something other than condemnation. Curiosity, at least, otherwise you wouldn't have called me. You wouldn't have come to see me.

You wanted me to re-tell this story, the story of your father, from my point of view. A woman's point of view. Of course, that's logical. You're a very young woman. You wonder what type of emotional life awaits you. How will it taste, how will it be seasoned? Will it satisfy you? Will it be sweet? Bitter? Or sour, which would be the worst.

You're afraid. We're all afraid.

Gigi talked a lot about you. I knew you from a distance. But I still knew you. The other day, when I saw you arriving at Titti's, I immediately knew what type of person you would be. Lively, intuitive, endowed with the same slightly instinctive intelligence as Gigi. Exactly as I saw you intuitively. Like all sensitive young women, you sense that the dominant discourse on love—prince charming, the *other half, made for each other*, as they say in magazines . . . —you sense that all of that is a myth. A great collective story. In Rome, as in Brussels, one out of two marriages end in shouting and wounds. What we call divorce.

By the way, I didn't ask you at Titti's if you had a boyfriend, a girlfriend, a partner, whatever? But it doesn't matter. I understand. I understand that you want to find out how you will be able to 'deal with' all of this. Gigi and Clara—that story which intrigues you—will it be able to offer you some keys?

I owe it to myself to be frank with you, Elvira. If I'm writing these notes, it's primarily for myself. To still be with Gigi a bit while putting him at a distance—I believe in the therapeutic virtues of writing, you see. Will you find something in these lines? You'll see for yourself. But keep in mind that this other way of loving, so different from the imposed models, can, without hurting anyone, make a woman happy.

From: Clara, clara.maturelove@alice.it
To: Gigi, gigi.maturelove@alice.it
Subject: *Diario di una mancanza*
Date: *5 ottobre 2014*

My darling, what do you think about something like that—as a preamble? Should I continue? Or am I writing completely for nothing? I don't want to upset your dear Elvira, either . . .

From: Clara, clara.maturelove@alice.it
To: Gigi, gigi.maturelove@alice.it
Subject: *Diario di una mancanza*
Date: *7 ottobre 2014*

Too bad. I'm going to continue. Maybe I'll see things more clearly, too, if I get to the end. One always writes to explain to oneself things that one doesn't really understand, right? Do you remember we discussed this? Was it at Marcello's or in

Greece? I'm beginning to mix things up, my God, it's terrible. No, I think it was on Skyros. Regardless, here is what I wrote to Elvira today.

For Elvira:

How did it begin? Exactly as Gigi describes. One evening, in Vienna. I don't really remember the concert in question any more. Rather, yes, but he neglected to mention it in his version. On the programme there was *Trois moments musicaux* by the young Danish composer, Jan Christiansen. From the beginning, something was wrong. I looked all around. Was there an echo in the hall? From where I was sitting, I heard the same musical phrases as on the stage, but slightly delayed. I finally figured out that it was a phone. A mobile phone was making that noise right in front of me. At the end of the first piece, I said something really angrily to the guy who was sitting in the row in front of me. But he assured me that he hadn't received a call. That's when Gigi gave me a truly terrified look. It was he. He had been looking for a video of that young composer before the concert and now his phone had turned on in his pocket, unbeknownst to him. I couldn't get over it. At that moment, it seemed stupid, and we laughed, as silently as possible, during the entire *deuxième moment*. Until Gigi signalled to me to leave, and he led me outside to drink some pink champagne. If one day you listen to the podcast of the programme I did for the RTBF on that Viennese concert, you'll notice that I never mention the *troisième moment musical*. And for good reason! In the taxi going home, Gigi forgot his phone.

Keep in mind that I could have done it. I mean, mention the *troisième moment*. Sometimes, as it happened, Gigi would encourage me to play truant. I would make a brief appearance at a press conference on a film shoot or whatever, and then I made up the rest. Gigi really enjoyed helping me. He always had the best ideas. In the end, I was thinking like Blaise Cendrars. Do you know that story, Elvira? When Cendrars published *Prose du Transsiberian*, the editor-in-chief of I don't know which French publication—Pierre Lazareff?—suspected that he had never set foot in Siberia. A fake travel tale, in sum. Cendrars got pretty upset. In the end, out of arguments, he lashed out at Lazareff: 'What the hell does it matter to you if I never took the Transsiberian . . . since I made it possible for all of you to take it!' Preferring fiction to reality. And always blending the two. That's exactly what Gigi and I were doing.

I have a vivid memory of the dinner that followed the concert. At the table, Gigi couldn't stop talking about his parents, his mother, their political involvement, and especially the mysterious death of his father. I understood that his father's death had nagged him constantly since childhood. Like a black hole around him, and into which he wandered without ever seeing the bottom of it. He talked about the PCI, of course, and the Italian Left. The state of the Left, yesterday, today, tomorrow . . . At that point, I had already zoned out. He whispered his room number in my ear, 443. And I slipped away. For a long time those numbers functioned like a code between us. 4-4-3. Sort of like the way one says '36' to order 'chicken with bamboo shoots' in a Chinese restaurant. 443. The rendezvous code. A rendezvous of love. That evening, however, we didn't really know where we were headed. Gigi had promised to follow my wishes. At least, that's what he told me later. We drank some Bordeaux. Château Lascombes 2004. Ripe, black cherry, full-bodied. Mature in your mouth. *Bliss.*

From: Clara, clara.maturelove@alice.it
To: Gigi, gigi.maturelove@alice.it
Subject: *Diario di una mancanza*
Date: *7 ottobre 2014*

Do you remember that bottle, Gigi? I can't remember, aside from the Sassicaia in Venice, ever drinking anything so good. I'll grant you, my memory is perhaps vaguely biased. The drunkenness of the first evening . . . But that's the way it is. You won't ever convince me that that Bordeaux wasn't exceptional. Petrus aside . . . OK. OK. I can feel that you're turning in your grave. I'm rambling. Maybe to delay the moment when, for Elvira, I'll enter into the meat of the subject? . . .

For Elvira:
Your father was a great hedonist. I'm repeating myself, you'll say. But it is always that word that first comes to mind when I think of him. A true lover of bodies.

Always fresh, natural and spontaneous. And then the simple acceptance that goes with it. I can see again the simplicity with which he threw his clothes down next to the bed, that first evening. I was amazed because, all the same, his body wasn't exactly youthful. It was that total absence of anxious self-consciousness that touched me. I should say, pleased me.

I was unbelievably surprised, because there is nothing like that in my culture. I come from the North, as you know. A country where we don't talk a lot. Brussels, in that regard, is like Copenhagen or even London. What is intimate, emotions, the inner life, all that is suspicious. But feelings are nothing next to the body, that great taboo. The very idea of the body is never to be mentioned. Talk about it to Ron, my husband. The word *lijf* in Dutch is almost a dirty word to him. Maybe because things of the body escape his control, and that lack of control is unacceptable to him?

So, I was stupefied to see a man of Gigi's age throw his clothes so joyfully into the air. I'm not saying that my own body has remained perfectly firm, but even so, I was shocked that he did that in front of me, the first time. With the light on. Without any covering. Because even if he was tall, tan and well 'preserved', as they say—I hate that expression, which makes me think of a forgotten bottle of old plums floating in alcohol—in short, even if his body might have had a powerful charm over me, he was still bearing, as you can imagine, the stigmata of the weight of his years.

To my surprise, Gigi's levity was contagious. Unlike him, I wasn't used to jumping into bed with a stranger like that. I say, unlike him, because, as I've told you, that's how I imagined him at the time. What a certain rumour had always spread about him in our circles. But how can I put it? What was bizarre is that I absolutely didn't care. Later, I continued to want to know nothing about his past, his affairs with other women, as well as the 'true' one. I didn't care about that which, often, is troubling, or even drives you crazy when you 'fall in love'. Don't ask me why. I don't deserve it. It was as if, suddenly everything had been relegated onto another plane of existence. A quickly forgotten dimension in which things once were important, but now, no longer.

That evening, in fact, all of that seemed unimportant. I caught myself acting just like him. I unbuttoned my skirt and took off my pantyhose with joyful abandon. Without guilt. Just desire. A very pure desire. I slipped under the linen sheets. It was new, and strangely familiar at the same time. As if our bodies were getting to know each other again. He must have had the same feeling. I remember he closed his eyes. And whispered these two words: '*Pure bliss.*'

I try to guess the questions you might have in reading these lines, Elvira. Maybe you're wondering about the difference in our ages? It's true, I've always been attracted to men with grey hair. Strange, isn't it? The weight of the years, sculpted faces, the web of wrinkles, grey hair, even bifocals . . . all of that is reassuring and attractive. With his great dominant male side, Gigi the Protector responded perfectly to that unusual tropism. But let's be clear: I wasn't looking for a father. As I said, it was all about pure desire. And Gigi understood this, too, he savoured each and every minute of our stolen love. A love that he had no longer expected, he told me one day while he was enjoying the moment, intensely. The way one delights in a child who comes late in life. The wonder is the same as for the firstborn. Because you know it will be the last.

I adored his shameless abandon. Later, I often compared him to a tree. I'm thinking about it as I'm writing this. I'm lying next to him holding his hard cock in my hand. We're under a harsh light. A Mediterranean light. 'You see,' I say to him, 'as long as I am attached to you like a branch, I will never fall.' He laughed when I said silly things like that. Then I would knead the silky skin of his thighs, bury my head in the soft folds of his stomach, resting it on the welcoming white hair at the bottom of his torso. I breathed him in. I breathed out. I felt everything in me relaxing. I had set down my suitcases. I had arrived somewhere.

Our relationship was dictated exclusively by that, the desire to be together. There were no issues of power, domination, sex or money. None of the usual things. Pure desire. When you're forty-six and almost seventy, and both people live with a partner they have no intention of leaving, things are ultimately pretty easy. Gigi and I had no expectations. Not that the other divorce, or that he or she be ever-present. On the contrary. With our professions, we were both used to having time to ourselves. Our children had left the nest and called on us only when they needed us. (Or when their bank accounts needed us. Don't deny it, dear Elvira, I know . . . But rest assured, it's the same thing with my sons.) We were both in good health, had time, money, the freedom to choose when and where we wanted to see each other, with no other goal, again, than that *pure bliss*. We hoped for nothing. We feared nothing. We were free.

I'm stressing that because in this world, that's what is perhaps the most subversive. 'Being' with an older person. Cheating on your fifty-year-old husband with a seventy-year-old man while expecting nothing from him. Creepy, wouldn't you say? We would agree on a date. We would get together. Often at his place in Sardinia, in that paradise that you know only too well and whose name he often asked me not to say in order to keep it for us. *Solo per noi.*

What about Ron, you're going to ask. What were things like with Ron, the other husband, the earlier one?

You have understood how much I loved him, but I sense that's not the meaning of your question. You want to know if he knew or not, what we said to each other and what we didn't, if we had a pact, like the one Sartre and Beauvoir had, the necessary and the contingent, and *tutti quanti*.

You know, Elvira, the older the relationship, the deeper it becomes. It becomes a very fluid mixture, a dough made of love, tenderness and respect. I won't give you a lecture. I just want to draw your attention to that old-fashioned idea of respect. You probably find it paradoxical that I talk about respect when I have just calmly sung the praises of polygamy. But there was a fierce determination between Ron and me not to hurt each other. And so, an ardent obligation not to let anything betray us. The old train ticket in a pocket, a hotel bill, credit-card receipt, a hair on a jacket . . . anything that would be compromising or impossible to justify if someone had inadvertently discovered it. No love letters, no photos. I won't say anything about the passwords and the obsession with *signing out*. It's a true discipline, you know. A cavalier attitude is fatal. Am I making you smile by insisting on such 'discipline'? Probably yes, at the idea that you really have to love your partner to 'cheat on' him that way, year after year, meticulously and reliably.

From: Clara, clara.maturelove@alice.it
To: Gigi, gigi.maturelove@alice.it
Subject: *Diario di una mancanza*
Date: *11 ottobre 2014*

My God! Now I'm telling your daughter very intimate things. What's come over me to confide in her like that? I think I should stop there. Especially since my second 'principle'—don't go into someone else's secret garden—goes completely without saying. The only difficulty is putting it into practice in these times of generalized intrusion. Computer, diaries, telephone, iPad, email, inbox, outbox, all sorts of correspondence . . . It's best not to touch it, the way one decides not to use drugs or drink alcohol. A simple matter of life hygiene. That willpower is developed, acquired, maintained. It becomes second nature. Each person understands that there is more to gain than to lose. I know that Irma and you, Gigi, were like that, too.

Only twice, but always unintentionally, Ron aroused my suspicions. The first time he was in New York, and I got it into my head to organize his desk. Without opening anything, without looking or reading. Just to make some piles and put some order to it. I came upon an old leather briefcase that seemed to be empty and so old that I thought about tossing it in the trash. To be on the safe side, I opened it. There was a box of rubbers in it. I closed it quickly. The box seemed new. I'll never know if it had been opened or not. When Ron got back home, I acted as if nothing had happened. How was New York? Had he seen *so-and-so*? . . . I always told myself, too bad for me, I shouldn't have gone into his office. Not to organize it, much less to throw out old briefcases. Sometimes I smile when I think that that briefcase is probably still there, behind the radiator. How many rubbers are gone from that box? I'll never know, and that's just fine.

And the second time? Did I ever tell you about it? Shall I? The second time was a Sunday morning. On Sunday, Ron played golf with his friends outside Brussels. Since he worked a lot during the week, I always said to myself that if he wanted to have affairs, it was the perfect cover. I didn't know the friends he golfed with, I didn't try to find out who they were, he had an entire morning without constraints. Free. Of course, I thought *in petto*, that would mean that his mistress would see him arrive every week with his Green's cap, his Bermuda shorts and his spiked shoes. Not very sexy. But, after all, what they were doing was sport, too. I mean, what they did when they got together. A different type of swing. Ron could even come home smelling like he had exerted himself, sweaty, jump into the bath, whistle in the shower, say he had had a good workout, and was hungry as a horse . . . nothing could be more normal. One time, though, one Sunday morning, while I was taking my time getting up, I heard an unfamiliar ping coming from the kitchen. I got up and looked for it. He had forgotten his iPad, which almost never happens. A text was posted. Cryptic and strange. *We must take care of this relapse. A fire and a few berries would do wonders.* Ron had been sick. Relapse, fire, berries? That was enough to intrigue me. Was I to imagine them naked in front of a fireplace, drowsy and crunching blueberries? I imagined that very kitsch scene with the golf bag not far away. And it didn't even bother me. Did it reassure me? (If Ron had a double life, too, then the symmetry was perfect and everything was in order?) I was almost more bothered by the fact—he never did it—that he could have forgotten his iPad. If his vigilance was relaxing, did it mean he loved me less? The message was posted on the screen along with a mobile phone number, which I didn't write down.

Then everything disappeared. The following Sunday, when he was getting ready to leave, I told Ron not to forget anything.

'What do you mean?' he asked.

I didn't usually act like a mother making sure that her little boy had his backpack and handkerchief.

'Your iPad,' I said. Don't forget your iPad.'

He didn't answer.

Dear Elvira,

Your father and I would often discuss the notion of secrets. The secret garden. How to maintain it, protect it from weeds, how not to trample on that of the other. As you can imagine, it quickly turned into a debate on the true and the false. The way in which we all live with lies.

On this subject, we didn't agree. Personally, I preferred opacity. I wanted people to lie to me—to protect me. Lying is being kind to the other . . . But Gigi demanded truth. At least as far as we were concerned. One day, I had called that 'the dictatorship of transparency'. The phrase made him mad.

Sometime after I had seen his film on Gramsci, I asked him why he hadn't included the episode that had so marked Gramsci when he was a child. I was referring to the way in which the little Tonio had discovered that his father, in 1900, had been put in prison. For *embezzlement and extortion,* as told in his biography. I loved those words I was little familiar with, but through which I guessed that it probably involved a not-very-serious matter of fraud. Gigi had told me that they had hidden from the young Gramsci that his father had been incarcerated, and that he hadn't been able to endure it. Similarly, in 1926, when he, too, was arrested by the Fascists—those who wanted to 'prevent his brain from functioning for twenty years', I love that phrase—so, when he was arrested and thrown into one of Mussolini's jails, Gramsci insisted that his son Delio know about it. He had been very upset to learn that his wife, in Moscow, had lied to him about it.

'But, Gigi, why didn't you put all that in your film? It's a moving story and very visual.'

'But too close to me,' Gigi had answered. 'It's somewhat my story, too. I never really knew how my father died. I sensed that my mother was hiding something from me. I was always being given different versions of his death. Like in *Rashômon*. One day the Fascists. One day the partisans. One day a crime of passion . . . In the end, I dropped it. It even occurred to me that my mother might have killed him in a fit of rage. That chilled me. I never heard her say, not once, that she missed him. Even today, I don't know . . . Should I have weighed down the film with everything that episode stirred up in me? Possibly. Maybe it would have been an opportunity to dive back into all that. A matter of seeing which dark images would have emerged. Focusing the camera on that darkness might have perhaps cured me . . . '

I could tell that he wasn't going to say anything else.

'In fact,' I pointed out to him, 'you've never really told me why you became interested in Gramsci. Because he was Italian?'

'No, no . . .' he protested. 'Today, Gramsci belongs to the world . . .'

'So?'

'For his concept of 'hegemony.' It is used in Europe by the Right to taunt the Left, but the Right doesn't really understand it. It thinks that it has beaten us for ever. In fact, you haven't read him . . .'

'Read whom? Gramsci? I did try once, but his writing was too elliptical. I dropped it. Anyway, political theory and me . . .'

'What mustn't be forgotten is that all his notebooks were written in prison, under extremely difficult conditions. Each sentence was looked at under a microscope and, once a week, a Fascist censor reported to Mussolini.'

'I see. That explains why he's not easy to read . . .'

'But I must say that he is understood better and better among the Anglo-Saxons. The English and the Americans in particular. Also the Indians. All those countries have produced academics who are Gramsci specialists and much more competent than ours here, in Italy—apart from the biography by Fiori that I used a lot for my film. Anyway, he had one of the most astute minds for European Marxism. A revolutionary. That's why nothing irritates me more than those opportunists who make use of him for any old purpose.'

'So, if I'm understanding you correctly, I should try reading him again?'

'Ah, well . . . It would be worth it . . . You'll see that he is completely contemporary. Especially today when the Left is so weak. For many in my camp, the 2008 Wall Street crash was a revelation. Billions were spent to save the system, as they say. So that those who govern the world could continue on their path, as if nothing had happened. Nothing changed. Or very little. Gramsci would have seen it as the perfect illustration of his famous concept of hegemony.'

Gigi continued, describing the development of the extreme Right, the scapegoats, but also the way in which we were taken in by the very rich, who had become, he said, 'monsters beyond anyone's reach'.

'This is exactly the mechanisms Gramsci alludes to when he describes the rise of Fascism in the Thirties. But, that's enough . . . enough Gramsci for one evening.'

'Why?'

'Because you're falling asleep.'

I wasn't falling asleep, but, it's true, I felt very far from all that. I didn't tell Gigi, but all that mythology, Marxism, comrades, even his vocabulary seemed from another age. That was the only thing about him, his political involvement, that left me . . . How can I put it? Not entirely with him. I admired him for it. And I found it just as endearing that he still believed . . . That he believed that one day… the revolution.

Once I tried to bring it up cautiously. But he immediately cut me off:

'You don't believe in it, I know.'

I laughed, defying him with a look:

'No, not for a moment.'

He had rolled his eyes, seeming to say: we'll see.

But what would we see? How could he not understand that he was fighting for a lost cause? Politics. Sometimes, to make him happy, I pretended to be interested in it. But, in my opinion, nothing was worse than politics—at least that which is carried out in our countries. That politics makes people obstinate, unjust, cruel and dogmatic. I didn't tell him, but he did sense what I thought. Again, he rolled his eyes:

'What if the rearguard battles were the battles of tomorrow?'

No, I didn't fall asleep listening to Gigi talk about Gramsci. I thought of other things. His 'Gramscianism' led me to my own family. To my great-grandfather in particular, a high-ranking officer who had suppressed the great Belgian strike of 1893. He had given the order to shoot the workers and he basked in the glory of it. It was an uncle—a brother of my father, but much older than he—who had told me the story. He remembered my ancestor congratulating himself for that 'victory' during a dinner with the bishop.

'Because, you see,' I said to Gigi, 'they were all devout Catholics in my family . . . Which didn't prevent one of my great-uncles from having participated actively in the war in the Congo.'

'Of course . . . one of the most horrible of colonial wars . . .'

Gigi was silent for a moment, then:

'Not many people know, but more than ten million Congolese died in it. Ten million, can you imagine? Killed by the Belgian landowners with the help of the army, in the first ten years of the twentieth century.'

'Horrific . . . And do you know what was in the office of that great-uncle in Brussels? A shrunken black hand. The hand of a worker who worked on a plantation. It was floating in a jar of formaldehyde, sitting on a shelf . . . That was my family. The coexistence of barbarism and civilization.'

'But, my dear, it has nothing to do with you. It's as if I were held responsible for Mussolini. But you were right to tell me . . .'

At that moment, I was holding his penis in my hand. It had become a ritual right before I fell asleep. I was about to close my eyes when I heard him laugh:

'Fortunately, you don't take after your great-uncle, because I wouldn't be able to sleep a wink all night.'

'What do you mean?'

'I would be too afraid to end up in formaldehyde.'

The next morning, when I pulled open the linen curtains, once again everything was white and pure. Inundated with light. I don't know why I told you all that. Why I went so far away from that, from that light. From that bliss. Sardinia. I had fallen madly in love with it, as you have guessed. To the point of loving the sun that burnt me and hurt the top of my back when I woke up. Gigi straddled my back on the white sheets and massaged my shoulders—red, much too red, I should cover myself today, put on a T-shirt at least—he massaged my shoulders, pressing with all his weight, with a nourishing oil made locally, something more or less secret and always organic that he bought in the village. An orange, some green tea. Coffee for him—but then, oh, he was at home, he made his coffee which was necessarily good, he couldn't complain as he did in Brussels or elsewhere and, finally, I didn't have to worry about that sacrosanct coffee—and then, light of heart, we went down to the beach.

Turquoise. Transparent. *Un po' fresca l'acqua?* No, no, wonderful. Are you coming? . . . He wore his plastic goggles so the salt wouldn't hurt his eyes.

You didn't know, you couldn't have known, but I often imagined you there. In 'our' cove. Gigi had told me that you swam like a mermaid. That the sea was your element, as it was his. I saw a photo of you in the house—I was going to write 'in our house' or 'at home'. I imagined you jumping on the white rocks, the way you must have done so many times when you were little—in particular, on the one that seems to have eyes and is smiling . . . The one that Gigi had baptized Poseidon. I saw you climbing like a mountain goat in the pine forest as far as Da Pietro. That must seem odd to you. You who were unaware of my existence. And I knew so much about you. But don't worry. Everything was full of goodwill. Gigi loved you so much.

He and I loved to order *polpo*. Grilled, of course—even if . . . we were being careful the past few years. Gigi claimed that octopus was full of cholesterol and, out of solidarity, I didn't eat it any more, either. We loved to eat fresh seabass and *vino rosso—Senti . . . un bicchiere di Cannonau . . . Non c'è problema.* He also said that Sardinian wines were not as good as Sicilian wine. That you could only drink them locally. Which we did. We would drink our Cannonau the way we would savour our story. In little sips. While biting into the *pane carasau* that Marcello brought us.

He knew my favourite *carasau*. The most fragrant. The one in which the little rosemary leaves are held in the dough and you see them inside like inclusions.

Sometimes we would talk about his favourite film-makers. Rossellini, Fellini, Visconti, Rosi, Pasolini, Pontecorvo, Antonioni.

'All geniuses,' said Gigi. 'I wonder whatever happened to that Italy. The Italy that was able to produce that cinema . . .'

We talked about De Sica's *Ladri di biciclette*. 'Pure innocence,' according to Gigi, who never watched it without a single, lone tear sliding down his cheek.

'What about Bertolucci?'

'His best is still *Il conformista*. I've always thought that you could transpose that film to today. You'd have to change the scenery and the costumes, but the dialogues, believe me, the dialogues would work just as they are.'

Sometimes we didn't talk. No need to furnish conversations. We would gaze around us. Looking at the edges of the foam or following the offshore line of the horizon. We would breathe in the sea, the jasmine. We would steal a grape from Pietro's trellis. Then we would go back to our house. Sorry—really—to *your* house. But I knew that Irma had not gone there for years. That she found the place too uncomfortable, too rustic, that she didn't love Sardinia, that she detested the islanders' accent, and that in the end she let Gigi go there alone. That made things easier for me, obviously. Coming back from Da Pietro, we would take a siesta, then we made love. Or the opposite. *Eravamo bene e basta.* It must surely seem idiotic to you. And it's true, when I think about it, there is nothing else to tell. *La gente felice non ha niente da dire.* How can I convey to you that plenitude which I don't remember ever being aware of at your age? We talk about love stories in the beginning and at the end. But we never tell about the middle. But that poetry of the middle is truly very beautiful. That feeling of fullness. Everything is there. All is well.

Not to expect anything, to hope for nothing. To be in the present and to savour it. Taste it all the better since you know it's ephemeral. Accept that it will end. One day. When? In a year? Two years? More? Gigi had created a password for his computer that made me laugh. It was the key to our private correspondence. Clara80. He never wanted to admit what that meant—out of embarrassment probably—but it seemed obvious to me. That Clara would be there until I'm eighty. What was most touching is that he had changed that password a few months after we met. After Clara80, it became Clara90. I had been *upgraded* in a sense. Could one still be 'together' at ninety and seventy? And what does that 'together' mean? What does such a late love look like?

What is most surprising in our case—we, ourselves, had trouble believing it—is that tenderness, laughter, companionship, had never, as might have been expected, supplanted the physical relationship. Our bodies were there. Pleasantly, peacefully there. For how much longer? And when they weakened? . . . We would find other games. I was sure of it. We loved life so much. Hearts and bodies, I had confidence in both. Gigi said the same thing, but secretly he prayed that his virility wouldn't abandon him. I wasn't worried.

It was a different idea that nagged at me. What if our liaison—I don't like that word, but what other term can I use? *Relationship* is so cold. And *love* . . . I sense that from being forced to repeat that word, I, the woman with greying hair, I'll end up making you laugh . . . Anyway, what if our liaison ended there, on that island, tomorrow, today, in an hour, during *la coccola*? For me, that was the nightmare. The absolute nightmare. That Gigi might have a heart attack. In Sardinia with me. In his house. *Nel letto.* Or elsewhere. At sea. I had tried so many times to get him to have a check-up. But he wouldn't hear of it. I know, he hadn't hidden from me that the possibility of his sinking to the bottom of the sea, one day while he was swimming far offshore, very far, didn't displease him. I think, deep down, he dreamt of that without admitting it to me. At ninety or in that water, literally. We would have made love—if one is still able to do it at that age, but that's another story. How can you know? There is hardly any 'literature' on that subject. Have you noticed? Love stories rarely grow old. I mean, the sexuality of the elderly is almost never brought up in our world. It's mentioned only to express the horror that, in nursing homes or Alzheimer clinics, the image of two 'uninhibited' old people elicits. But what about when the protagonists are of sound mind? . . . Two happy old people in love—*Deux vieux heureux et amoureux*? That's funny—in French it rhymes . . . The words seem to want to go together. But not the ideas. Maybe you think that, too? Maybe at this point in your reading you're already disgusted? You're angry at me for shoving this in front of you? Gigi's love affair with an unknown woman who could be your mother. A hidden love combined with an elderly love. Horror times two!

From: Clara, clara.maturelove@alice.it
To: Gigi, gigi.maturelove@alice.it
Subject: *Diario di una mancanza*
Date: *15 ottobre 2014*

My dearest Gigi, my darling, my love. The reason I haven't written to you for a week is that I went back to Belgium. This evening, I'm alone in Vollezele. It's a shame you never came to our country house. Vollezele, the Brabant. Rural Flanders. At this hour, a warm light casts coppery rays on the oaks. Do you remember the little terraced apple trees I planted? You taught me the name in Italian. *Spaliera? Spalliera?* Anyway. They're covered with fruit this year. For the first time. This evening, after my detox soup—I know, you're going to shriek—I'm going to slip under the covers and I'll continue to write down some notes for Elvira. Will she be interested at all in what I've written so far? I have no idea. But really, my Gigi, you should see this light. Even your lighting specialist, the champion of the world in chiaroscuro, the maestro of contrasts—who was he? I've forgotten his name . . . Paolo?—even he wouldn't be able to create these golds that stream down the branches in the garden.

From: Clara, clara.maturelove@alice.it
To: Gigi, gigi.maturelove@alice.it
Subject: *Diario di una mancanza*
Date: *16 ottobre 2014*

Gigi amore, it's not easy to break off. Here, in Vollezele, I no longer know where I am. Impossible to write today. It wouldn't come. I decided to sleep with the window open. Usually, when I'm alone in this house, I listen to Schubert's 'Lieder'. Or Bach, Bach and more Bach, on a crackling turn-table from the Eighties. An old machine missing a lot of its parts, you would hate it. But this time I preferred to think of us with, for a single soundtrack, tunes for solo owl in the darkness. And while it was hooting at full volume, memories arose out of the shadows. Your words.

'I would have never thought of that . . . '

'What?'

'That the last love could have the strength of the first . . . '

'*You're getting sentimental, darling.* Be careful!'

'No, no, what I wonder is if our situation is rare or if people don't talk about it . . . '

'We'll never know . . . anyway, it's crazy when you think about it.'

'What?'

'All those essential questions to which we'll never have answers . . . '

We had already had that conversation. It came back to me now, I had told you the story of my friend Elena who had come to spend the weekend here in the Brabant. Elena didn't seem well. She was thin, weak. At first, she told me she was 'a little depressed', like that, out of the blue.

'You know how it is. You don't insist in those cases. You were raised well. But that time, I don't know, I was fed up with good manners, with reserve, politeness and niceties. You must believe, my dear Gigi, that you had begun to rub off on me. I wanted to dig into all that like in a molehill in the garden. A kick with your rubber boots, you scrape the dirt with your foot, and see the entrance to the hole. The beginning of the secret . . . I opted for the intrusive way. I'm a journalist, after all . . .'

'What happened?'

'Elena ended up telling me she was going through a period of agonizing doubt. Did Sebastian—her lover—love her less now? Wasn't he different, less eager, less joyful, less passionate, was he going to leave her, should she get in front of it, would she let herself be humiliated, if only I knew how much she loved him, but she loved Luc, too . . . In any event, she wasn't sleeping, wasn't eating much. I asked how long it had been going on. Well, it had been going on for years, old man—sorry, Gigi . . . "*mon vieux*" is a very French expression. Rest assured, dead or alive, I would never have called you that. And so, it had been going on for years. What surprised me was not her affair. It was the amount of time. All those years we had talked without *saying* anything. And we were friends?'

'So close, yet so distant . . . is that what you mean?'

'Yes. It was dizzying. Words that are there to take up space. To decorate . . .'

'We never really know anyone . . . That's a fact.'

'Even in Italy? Even women when they get together? Here, there's a perimeter—lovers, loving habits, suffering, ecstasy, the fear of being abandoned, cheated on, the fear of cheating or of having the wrong partner, the fear of being judged, shame, the way in which one loves to take or be taken, kissed, caressed, the words one likes to hear, the torturing anguish, is he thinking of me, does he have someone else . . . all of that, that is, in the end, what is most essential, all that is a forbidden private property—do not enter—barbed wire—danger zone. All of that is masked by the parts that we play and play to ourselves.'

'You make me laugh, my Clara. You were the first to be shocked the first evening when I . . .'

'Oh, no, that was different. You weren't pulling any punches. We hardly knew each other. We were having dinner for the first time and you asked me . . . '

'How had I put it?'

'*Do you still menstruate?* Rather direct, wouldn't you say? I was dumbfounded. I thought—he wants to know how old I am. I'm still on the right side of the mirror. What an asshole!'

'A misunderstanding, *darling*. Misunderstanding. I told you later why I asked you that. I was so madly in love. I wanted a child. Just like that. Right away, yes. And I've wanted that child for a long time, you know . . . '

'But Gigi, you were aware, more or less, of my age . . . '

'And a lot of progress is being made in that domain these days. Especially in this country.'

'When I think about it again now, I'm touched . . .'

'. . . We had even thought about having it carried by a surrogate mother.'

'In Costa Rica, or someplace. We asked each other for news when we saw each other. Like that, as a game . . .'

'Regardless, at the time, I know what you were thinking—should I slap him and walk out? Dot the 'i's? Show this oafish Dago what I'm made of?'

'I must have stammered, "*Yes I do*," blushing. But I should have answered you with just as good. Ask you if you had prostrate issues or could still get it up.'

'As for that, my dear, I answered you . . . '

'That's cute. In any case, what is certain is that that conversation had set the tone for our relationship.'

'On the very first night we had broken all barriers, cut the barbed wire, as you say. We began to talk about everything.'

'*Everything under the sun*. That's what you said. Why is all that coming back to me? What was your question?'

'Seventy-somethings and the autumn sun.'

'Oh, yes. The false tough ones like you. Those who rediscover at a ripe old age the emotions of their first love. And who can't get over it . . . You wondered if there were more than you might believe. I said we'd never know.'

'And you were right. *Clara aveva ragione. A-ve-va ragione . . .*'

'Oh, *please*, Gigi, *stop it.*'

'*Perché*? I'm writing a little song to the glory of my Clara. Don't tell me she doesn't like to be right?'

I shrugged. You took me in your arms. You whispered, '*Bliss.*' You again said you were surprised that old age is the best time for love. Because it was deep and light at the same time. One is rid of all that one might have to prove. One could finally breathe, savour, laugh.

I can still hear you:

'The older we get, the more fun we'll have, my Clara!'

You also said that if one day our 'light years', as you called them, became a film, it could be called that. *Pure Bliss.* Or simply *Bliss. Gioia. Joie.*

'*Che ne pensi?*'

From: Clara, clara.maturelove@alice.it
To: Gigi, gigi.maturelove@alice.it
Subject: *Diario di una mancanza*
Date: *17 ottobre 2014*

My dearest Gigi, my very own,
A thought occurred to me. If I had a single idea to transmit to your daughter—but no, in fact, it's not that, it isn't an *idea*. It's even the opposite of an idea. If I had one single thing to get her to feel—feel closely, sense—it would be that, *la gioia* . . .

That she have an intuition for it. Like something hidden behind things. The secret of secrets. I know what you're thinking. I can hear you from here. 'Commonplace. Pathetically commonplace.' But wait. I'm not done.

From: Clara, clara.maturelove@alice.it
To: Gigi, gigi.maturelove@alice.it
Subject: *Diario di una mancanza*
Date: *18 ottobre 2014*

Do you remember? You told me about it, you and Nadia. The incident in the car. Elvira wasn't yet in high school. She had seen you when she was getting out of school. She had smiled, she was radiant. Then she had seen Nadia and her smile froze. She had become livid. Had dropped her backpack and run off.

    'So? . . . '

Then you had told me too that, after that, Elvira quickly modified your Wikipedia page. That, in the 'biography' part she had, without mentioning it to anyone, added this: *Giangiacomo G. is married to the academic Irma T. They have two children.* Be careful, potential admirers. Gigi, my father, is anything but free. Move along. There's nothing to see. With Irma, my mother, they live happily and have children. *The end of the story.* Like in fairy tales. And your Elvira truly needed a fairy tale on men and women at that time. She was what, thirteen? Fourteen? She had figured out the password to your computer. It wasn't difficult. She just had to paste Gramsci or Trotsky to your birthdate. By trying several combinations, she fell on the right one. She read your email. Probably twice. So that when a woman was being a bit too insistent, she told her to get lost. *FUCK OFF*, she had suggested to one of the others. The woman at the other end of the email was thunderstruck. When you found out, you all laughed. Irma had even bothered to write to excuse her daughter's 'adolescent fit'. You see, Gigi, I'm sure that those incidents have left a subconscious mark on Elvira that is much deeper than you think. I know, I know, you're going to make fun of me. You're a small-time psycho-analyst . . . But how can you think that those adolescent traumas didn't affect the future woman? That model—so pitiful, so ordinary—that anti-model, I should say, you imposed it on her. You, society . . . Afterwards it stuck with her. Something tells her men are traitors. That women are consumable and disposable. That the day will come when she, herself . . . the famous expiration date . . . the EDCW (expiration date for the consumption of women). When I think of that, I want to vomit. The same little voice tells her that, like her mother, she, too, will be betrayed. Because it's inevitable. Because that's the way men are. She tells herself that she will be betrayed, and she will suffer. Well, in a certain way, your Elvira is already suffering. She's suffering without knowing it. That's why I feel compelled to write to her.

From: Clara, clara.maturelove@alice.it
To: Gigi, gigi.maturelove@alice.it
Subject: *Diario di una mancanza*
Date: *18 ottobre 2014*

Wait, I'm going to digress. Look at what I found this morning in *De Morgen*. A dating site called BeautifulPeople.com, which has more than a million members, was just attacked by hackers.

As its name indicates, BeautifulPeople.com is reserved for BP, 'beautiful people', as my sons would say. If you want to sign up, you will have to send your precise measurements, waist size, chest size, maybe even the length of your penis for men, who knows, oh yes, of course, and lots of recent photos . . . After which they classify you in a range of possible categories from *Absolutely Not* to *Beautiful*. On the newspaper page, a sampling of the happy elect illustrates the article. Six women in swimsuits, in-between them, a large, muscular Black man who is flexing his pecs and holding out his large, muscular arms to them. Keep in mind, you're not accepted by BeautifulPeople in perpetuity. This year, five thousand people were kicked out because they had gained weight after Christmas. Real follow-up, you see. Serious work. But, what's funniest, is the hacking. A virus called Shrek inserted a bunch of ugly people into the system. *That's what alerted us*, explained James Brown, Managing Director of BeautifulPeople. *Because those thousands of new members were anything but Apollos* (in Dutch there is an amusing expression which says that they are not 'subjects for an oil painting'). On behalf of the site, the director presented his excuses. *It's harsh to have led* (all those ugly people) *to believe that they were beautiful,* he said. *At least they will have had a little slice of paradise. It's better than never having tasted it at all.* And all of that because of the horrible Shrek with his apple-green head and his funnel-shaped ears. I can hear you from here: 'Love in the twenty-first century—instant, zapping, narcissistic . . . ' And you would add: '*Pathetic. Really pathetic.*' Gigi, I've forgotten. You'll never guess the slogan of BeautifulPeople: *Life is short—have an affair.*

Fine. Do you find my 'story of the day' stupid? No more—and even less—than your Cow Sex in Bali, *my dear*. I tell myself that Elvira's generation is caught between two bad options. On one side there is the old monogamous model, with its parade of hypocrisy and suffering. On the other, it's just as stupid: *Life is short—have an affair*. It's not too crazy, really, to seek another path.

From: Clara, clara.maturelove@alice.it
To: Gigi, gigi.maturelove@alice.it
Subject: *Diario di una mancanza*
Date: *19 ottobre 2014*

If this were an exam question, it would be: 'Can a woman love several men without betraying any?' I'd like to provide your Elvira with some weapons. Weapons to reconcile everything. Loving involvement and freedom. I'd like her to understand that a woman who sincerely loves 'her' men takes care of them, thinks of them, worries about them, that that woman has nothing to do with *Life is short—have an affair*. That it's in fact the exact opposite. I'd like her to know that you can be faithful in infidelity.

I never talked to you about François, one of my most devoted 'cicisbeos'. I know, I know, the very word immediately turns you off. I can see you swearing to your great gods: 'I will never be a cicisbeo, Clara! *Mai. Mai. Mai . . .*' Fine, but that's not what it's about. In this case, François had adopted two children. First a boy, then a girl. When the little girl arrived, the son was upset and jealous. 'Imagine that you're on a beach,' his father told him. 'It's sunny. Another child arrives and sits down not far from you. Will it be any less warm then? Will there be less sun?'

I often think about that. About the quantity of sun. I don't see why what is a given for filial love can't apply just as well to all love. You laugh? Are you worried? Explain to Elvira that monogamy is an illusion? To do the same thing with prince charming as with Santa Claus? It's tricky, I know. It scares me a little, too . . .

OK. I'm going to go down and make a cup of tea.

From: Clara, clara.maturelove@alice.it
To: Gigi, gigi.maturelove@alice.it
Subject: *Diario di una mancanza*
Date: *26 ottobre 2014*

Talking about the quantity of sun, you won't believe it . . . I couldn't resist, if you can imagine. All it took was an ad on my screen. A *low-cost* flight for Cagliari. And that was it. I told myself a little light to end the autumn . . . I went off like that, on a whim.

I did hesitate a bit, as you might guess. The idea of seeing everything again. Of seeing it all alone... In the end, I found the key under the flat stone, as if your house didn't know a thing. As if it was waiting for us, for our traditional secret voyage, our little 'Mediterranean shoot'.

In Brussels, I said I was going to do an interview with Ettore Scola. Maybe his last. That convinced them . . . In the end, Scola wasn't well, which I had anticipated and which avoided my stopping in Rome. Instead, I saw Giulio Capitta, you know, the Sardinian director. Not exactly the same thing, but I had to come back with material. I'm sure he would have got on your nerves. You would have said, '*pieno di sè*'— '*full of himself*', And it would have been your final word. *Pieno di sè*. Can we say that in French, too, '*plein de lui-même*'? I wonder if there are people empty of themselves . . .

Me, perhaps? At that moment, the moment of seeing everything again without you, I was very afraid of being empty of my substance. Of being liquefied. But no, I was strong, you would have been proud. It was a close call. Three days going back and forth from one state of mind to another, my heart clinching, my heart joyful. Between enthusiasm and sadness, my soul followed the undulations of the hills of myrtle and juniper. I opened all the windows in the house. The light was white. The curtains white. The walls white. Everything was pure. I talked to you, you were there. I thought of what Proust wrote in *Les Plaisirs et les Jours*: *Isn't absence, for the one who loves, the most certain, the most effective, the liveliest, the most indestructible, the most faithful of all presences?*

And the most athletic, too? Proust couldn't have suspected, but just imagine that I brought you down to the beach on a bike! Not our usual cove, I didn't want to take any risks. Especially not to run into Marcello. No, it was the little Calla Cipolla beach. 'Beautiful onion'! You remember? The one you get to by a pothole-filled, bumpy dirt path. The lagoon, the pink flamingos, the turquoise water, the white sand, the junipers . . . It was late in the season but, after riding the bike, the sea wasn't that cold.

On the way back, I took a bus. I know, you would have grumbled again:

'A bus to Cagliari? *My very own woman* . . . why not a taxi?'

'Because it's much more fun to watch the people who get in and out. You always loved that, too.'

After some time, I thought the bus would never come. I was the only one at the bus stop, on the road, in the middle of the dunes. Like in *La Mort aux trousses*. A car went by every ten minutes. I could follow the sound of its engine for a long time, then nothing. *Silenzio*. A fly or two, drowsy, flew in the warm air. I saw myself abandoned on this wild coast. Missing my plane. I tried to come up with an excuse for home and the office.

Then, what they call the Pullman here arrived. Next to me there was a little, old woman you would have liked. A black scarf on her head, gold earrings, and wrinkled like a fig. When the bus took off, she made the sign of the cross. I told myself that, like this part of the island, she had escaped modernity. But at that very moment, something rang. It was her mobile phone. Intergalactic sounds. Music from *Star Wars*. It rang twice and, both times, she waited before answering, staring at the object with a strange look, as if Darth Vader, or some other extraterrestrial, was challenging her in person. Then she lowered her scarf, uncovering her left ear, said a few short words which I couldn't understand, and hung up.

Was it her husband who was following her? She seemed strong and lofty like the Sardinian peasants you often described.

You said that thing that had made me laugh, I remember. You had said: 'I come from a *densamente matriarcale* family.' Densely matriarchal. We started talking about matriarchy. Not only in Sardinia. You talked about the Naxis in China. Told me that there, in the Yellow River valley, the women live with their brothers and don't have a permanent husband. Men visit them at home at night, sexual relations are free and they keep the children. Then you launched into Engels. *The Origin of the Family*. You must have told me that it was the same with the Iroquois. Or I don't know where, in Timbuktu, perhaps, in the early days of Islam. Or in southern Kerala . . . I can still hear you:

'A wife could tell her husband that she was going away for a while to live with another man. When she returned, the husband didn't say a thing. What do you think of that, my Clarinette?'

A new nickname? You were always making them up for me. What did I think? Images of little Greek houses went through my mind. I told you again that I loved Ron and that I would never leave him. But that I would love to spend six months with you, Gigi, in that white hiding place with a vineyard and reed screens. Just on the beach. Just six months. What are six months, over the span of a life? I asked:

'How do you say "polygamy" for a woman? "Polyandry", is that it?'

You didn't answer. I continued to think out loud:

'At home, a man who loves women is a *womanizer*, a Don Juan or whatever. In any case, he's someone that other men

envy or admire. Whereas a woman who loves men is necessarily a whore.'

'A classic remark, my Clara . . . Where are you going with
it?'

I reflected without saying anything.

'Well?'

'Well, other women are the first to condemn her,' I said.
'But you'll note that there is always a point on which everyone
seems to agree. It's the famous assertion according to which
"men and women aren't the same". Don't you find that
bizarre?'

'Not at all,' you said, frowning with your bushy eyebrows.

'What do you mean, not at all?'

'Clara *cara* . . . It's obvious that it's very convenient for
men to assert that "men and women are different". That
allows them to retain their power. Especially when women
themselves pass on the idea.'

'I'm happy you admit it.'

'But I've told you a hundred times that Engels, like Marx,
moreover, saw women as "the primary oppressed class". Don't
make me repeat everything you call my old-fashioned ideas.'

'Ah, yes, no, please.'

'I told you the story of my friend Stefano?'

And it went on. And on . . .

You always had a thousand anecdotes. Sometimes—
often—I already knew them, but I let you tell them again.
Without interrupting you. You so enjoyed telling them. I

wondered where you got all your stories. How much you embellished them. And why. Your interest in matriarchy, could it have a connection to your father's death?

That's where I was in my thoughts when a group of five young Africans got in the bus. We were getting close to the industrial park of Macchiaredu. On the right of the road, the sea was sparkling. Little squares of blue appeared and disappeared between the pine trees. On the left, there was the lagoon, land and water mixed together. Two flamingos were flying in a line. The female behind the male? Mentally, I baptized them Euphoria and Melancholia. I watched them as long as I could. Pink and black. Two tiny spots in the sky.

Two tiny spots in the sky and then nothing.

*

When I returned home to Brussels, Ron was charming. Loving, even. I don't know why but, once again, I couldn't help thinking that he knew.

I was always apprehensive when I returned home. A bit of guilt? The fear of being found out? But this time I didn't have anything to feel guilty about. I had indeed been in Italy, but you weren't there. Not in flesh nor in bones. So what did I fear? Maybe that. Only that. 'Going home'. To the port or from a trip. In a row or the right path. You had trouble with the French word 'rentrée'. You saw it as 're-entry'. And that became a habit. You would send me an email: *How was your re-entry?* As if every time I was penetrating into a new dimension. Another story. Walking through walls of feelings.

I would write: *Re-entry good. Tutto bene.* YLH. I didn't dare tell you that, on my first night back, we went out to dinner with X, Y or Z—I knew that that would annoy you. You wanted me to remain in the bubble, with you, as long as possible. And I didn't dare tell you, either, that I wasn't unhappy to see them. That I was content with my lives. All my lives. Because, in truth, there isn't just one life in life, you were well placed to know that . . . In fact, if one day I give Elvira these notes, I must remember to tell her that I tweaked the Unamuno quote. *Because what you want is this life, and that one, and another—you want them all.* Father Miguel's phrase usually ends there. The '*And you are quite right*' is my addition. Why should one life chase away another?

That evening, in Brussels, I had a strange dream. Upsetting. But how can I describe it? Both more and less upsetting than I might have imagined—I, myself, perceived that ambiguity in my sleep. Ron was admitting to me that he had had an affair in the past. But it was, in his words, 'more than an affair'. A relationship with a woman that resulted in the birth of a child. A hidden child. He told me that very matter-of-factly, quickly, not entirely as an aside, but almost. At the end of a sentence, in the kitchen, just as we were about to sit down to dinner. I was stupefied. You really don't know a person. But there, I was indeed forced to admit that the dark side of Ron was better hidden than I could ever have expected. Above all, my husband had gone well beyond what I, myself, had experimented with. I, who had always considered myself uncanny, different . . . What a mistake! What a joke! And my pseudo-theory on the art of lying was sincere. Not only must he have practiced multiple acts of infidelity, but next to his parallel life, my transversal loves suddenly seemed completely banal to me.

I thought again of all the stupid things one can keep repeating to oneself about one's spouse. Out of a lack of knowing him. Or out of blindness. What I called his very Flemish caution regarding the body, for example. Never would I have expected this. The affair, as you can guess, didn't cause any problems. But the child . . . Ron's passing to the act went beyond my own schemas. And even yours, Gigi. Do you remember? We had talked a thousand times about that imaginary child we dreamt of having together. Who was going to be born in Costa Rica by a young, surrogate mother. We had gone very far in our fantasy. But neither of us had ever set foot in San Jose.

Still in my dream, I picked up my phone and tapped your number in Rome. I wanted to talk to you. So that you, Gigi, would clarify things for me. So you would give me your male point of view. Only you could do it. Did Ron have a problem with reality? Had he imagined that something was not truly true as long as it remained absolutely secret? I slowly tapped the numbers . . . 0-0-3-9 . . . It rang and rang. I hung up. Something wasn't right. I suddenly remembered you were dead.

But the dream still continued. Ron was telling me: 'We could pretend it is a child from an earlier marriage. Then it wouldn't change anything.' I thought: Well, let's see . . . He added that he would love me for ever. 'For ever my Clara.' And explained a theory—which greatly resembled that of François—on the amount of sun. I wondered where he had heard it. In the end, we fell asleep.

The next day (still in the dream), Ron seemed joyful to me. He said something like:

'You are golden, my love. The Mediterranean did you good.'

The Mediterranean had done me good, but everything seemed bizarre. Deeply bizarre. Even I, I wasn't my usual self. Not only stunned but nauseous. Morning sickness, as if . . . But it was difficult to believe.

So I locked myself in the bathroom. I did a quick calculation. The date of your death. The last time we had been together. Was it possible. It was.

In a tailspin, I returned to bed. Ron and I made love. He kept saying he loved me. That he would love me for ever. In perpetuity. I told him, me too. I was sincere. Moved, too, you can imagine. And I found that a sort of parity had been re-established.

From that time, curiously, everything was very good between Ron and me. Better and better, even. Our relationship became much more profound. That's how the dream ended. But I see myself again ultimately thinking that the absurd dream wasn't a nightmare. Because it ended on a joyful note. Follies attract and ignite each other, I said to myself. The people with whom you live, those who attract you, don't appear by chance. Perhaps even, deep down, we're all the same. We move along masked and naked. And all our stories are equal, because there is always only one. That of time that passes by.

When I woke up—really, this time—I turned to Ron. It seemed to me that he was smiling in an unusual way.

Later in the morning he asked me offhand:

'How's your Italian friend? . . . '

'Which one?' I answered vaguely.

'Your friend . . . you know . . . the filmmaker . . . the Roman filmmaker, Giangiacomo G., that's his name, isn't it?'

'Ah, yes . . . '

'What ever happened to him? Did you see him over there?'

'. . . He passed away.'

'Oh . . . '

There was a brief silence. A very slight trembling.

Then Ron added, smiling:

'By the way, my Clara, I have two tickets for this evening . . . Two tickets for the opera . . . *Un ballo in maschera* . . . '

* * *